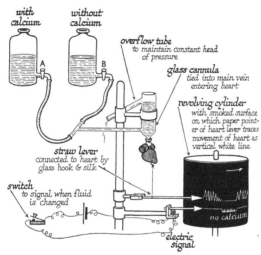

FIG. 433.—SET-UP OF EXPERIMENT TO SHOW THE DEPENDENCE OF THE HEART-BEAT ON METALLIC IONS

THE ANIMAL SCIENCES

RON HOTZ

COACH HOUSE BOOKS

first edition

Published with the assistance of the Canada Council for the Arts
and the Ontario Arts Council

We also acknowledge the Government of Ontario through the
Ontario Book Publishers Tax Credit program and through
the Ontario Book Initiative.

NATIONAL LIBRARY OF CANADA CATALOGUING IN PUBLICATION

Hotz, Ron, 1964-
    The animal sciences / Ron Hotz.

ISBN 1-55245-122-4

    I. Title.

PS8565.O7595A76 2003   C813'.6   C2003-902951-4
PR9199.4.H65A66 2003

for Evelyn

I

'Where is he?' asked Duffer.

Kookla was lying with her back on the floor. She didn't respond. Instead, she focused her attention on Luigi, the black rabbit who rested quietly on her chest. She adjusted her position slightly in order to accommodate the rabbit's weight and released a rolling nickel from her pant pocket. The nickel meandered across the studio floor. Duffer stamped a foot over it.

'Listen,' he said. 'I need to find Robin.'

Kookla ignored him. Duffer sat down cross-legged on the floor opposite her. She pulled down on the rabbit's soft ears.

'Before I came in I overheard you talking with somebody,' Duffer continued. Kookla's bottom lip trembled. 'Were you talking with Robin? Did he call you?' She stroked the rabbit's downy fur until its tiny pink eyes blinked slowly to sleep. 'Maybe you were talking to yourself … or maybe to Luigi?'

'Go away,' she said.

'Not until you help me find Robin.'

Kookla tipped her head to one side and looked at Duffer. Her eyes were different colours. One iris was green and the other blue. The lids were moist but he didn't think she'd been crying. She watched him with little interest. He feigned indifference and occupied himself with a button on his overcoat.

'My friend who works security at the hospital caught Robin stealing from the antiquary,' Duffer said. Kookla looked surprised.

'Robin got away but my friend had to notify the police. I just wanted to let him know that the police might be looking for him.'

'When did this happen?'

'About a week ago.'

'Why are you telling me now?'

'Because I just found out about it.'

Kookla frowned and looked at the studio clock. It was on a table next to an aquarium that held a pile of water toys and a giant goldfish named Attila. The clock's display was flickering 2:04 a.m.

'Why are you telling me this at two in the morning?' she glared. Her tone awakened Luigi. He sat up, sniffed the air and lay down with his head on Kookla's shoulder.

'You can turn off the high beams,' he said. 'I'm leaving.' Duffer unfolded his legs and raised himself off the floor. 'I thought this was important.' He turned his back to Kookla and opened the door.

'Before you go I want to ask you something.'

Duffer released the door handle and looked at her.

'What would you have done if Autumn was here?'

He thought for a moment. 'Are you and Autumn back together?'

Kookla pressed a cheek into Luigi's fur. The pressure released a thread of tears into the soft pile of his winter coat.

The Coat Check Diner was open twenty-four hours a day and was situated in the city's industrial west end. Autumn had learned that he could sit in a booth for hours so long as he continued to order fresh coffees. It was two in the morning. The waitress had served him his last cup of coffee at midnight. Autumn stretched out his legs and relaxed into the wounded red vinyl of the seat. The formica table surface, slick to the touch, allowed his mug to slip from hand to hand without disturbing the level of the coffee.

Autumn dipped his head toward the mug and took a sip. The coffee was cold. He had been sitting there for a long time.

The table was dressed with a ketchup bottle, salt and pepper shakers, a metal napkin dispenser and a paper menu. Autumn removed a black pen from his shirt pocket and doodled on the menu. The waitress walked over and asked if he needed anything else.

'No thank you,' he said.

The waitress ripped a bill from her pad and placed it face down on the table. She stood there for a moment and looked at his drawing. 'Don't write on the menu,' she told him.

'He is much with a bad habit,' said a voice.

Igor was standing next to the table. His pockmarked face was smiling. A smoking cigarette was hanging from his lip.

'Do you want to order something?' asked the waitress.

'No,' replied Igor. He sat down in the booth facing Autumn and searched the table for an ashtray. The waitress retrieved a brimming ashtray from a nearby table and walked away.

'Thank you, Miss,' he called after her.

Igor had immigrated from a riverside Latvian town named Riga. He had worked there as a mechanical engineer developing gasoline-efficient tractor engines. Later on, with the assistance of a grant from his polytechnical institution, he developed an inexpensive high-caloric ceramic engine. At the age of thirty-four, after he had attained a full professorship, he moved to North America. Unfortunately, the universities and industries he approached refused to acknowledge his credentials. He was, however, qualified to work as a garage mechanic. Igor worked in various grease pits for several years until he had saved up enough money to open his own garage. He had met Autumn through Kookla when she had worked in his garage.

'Breakfast?' Igor asked. He tapped his cigarette ash into the ashtray. He was wearing a pair of brown gloves. The first and second fingers of the glove were nicotine stained.

'No, just a coffee. It's too early for breakfast.'

'I had breakfast here before,' he said. 'A soft-boiled egg.' He stopped and motioned for Autumn to move in closer. 'It was too soft … ' Igor removed his gloves. The fingernails were nicely manicured although residue from the oil pans had discoloured them. Again, the first and second fingers were stained with nicotine. 'I knocked the little cap off my egg with a spoon and looked inside.' His hands reproduced the tableau with puppet-show enthusiasm. 'And what do you think I found?' Autumn shrugged. 'The white of the egg was not yet cooked and in the middle of the yellow … it was alive.' Autumn frowned. 'For long time I watched this beating heart inside egg. It ticked away breakfast time. Such a funny thing to happen, don't you think, how heart survived hot water?' Autumn nodded.

Igor then associated the very soft-boiled egg with an article he had written for *The Journal of Science*. It was a prospectus on the development of a friction-free glass engine with a double atrium and ventricle system. Autumn listened carefully. Igor understood that his friend was just being polite.

'I am leaving,' Igor said. He inhaled the last breath of his cigarette and drilled out the butt. He then put his gloves on and stood up from the table. 'Please give my love to Kookla.'

'I will the next time I see her.'

Igor tightened his scarf around his neck. 'The next time you see her? Are you no longer together?'

'It's hard for me to say.'

Igor settled back into the seat. 'What happened?'

Autumn resumed his doodling. 'I don't really know.'

'So where are you to stay?'

Autumn shook his head. 'I can't stay with Kookla … not after tonight.'

'Then you are to stay with me,' he said. 'I am to insist.'

Autumn looked up from his drawing. 'Are you sure?'

'Do not be an idiot.' Igor lifted Autumn's coat from off the boothside hanger. 'Here,' he said, throwing the coat onto Autumn's lap. 'Let's go.'

Autumn smiled. 'Where are we going?'

'First we are to make with a prits.'

'To make with a what?' Autumn capped his pen and placed it in his shirt pocket.

'A *prits*, it is the same as a *banya* … no, the word *banya* is in Russian. How do you say a word in English for where men go to make a steam?'

'A steam bath?'

'Yes.'

'How are we getting there?'

'*Skaistā temprementāla cẹla mīlākā*. The Beautiful and Temperamental Mistress of the Road,' he translated.

'Oh no,' recalled Autumn. 'That car almost got me killed.'

'No, it did not.'

'Well, it almost got me arrested.'

'When is this?'

'Almost a year ago. It was late at night – you offered me a lift back to my studio, and then you made me stand lookout while you stole parts from parked cars.'

'I remember this now,' laughed Igor. 'You were very upset.'

'I was upset because the police started chasing us.'

'But we got away.'

'We got away because you smashed your car into the police cruiser.'

'My friend,' he smiled, 'such an accident is on purpose. The Mistress is too slow to make away from a police cruiser. That is why instead of accelerating forward I had to reverse my beautiful girl into police car. The terrible crash was to make for the airbags to explode. *Boom!* The police car cannot drive and the police cannot get out of car.'

Autumn stood up from the booth and flipped over the bill. He put some money on the table. 'While the cops struggled and swore and tried to get out of their car you just stood there and finished your cigarette.'

'They were not hurt.'

'They were not happy.' Autumn put on his coat. 'Tell me something. It's pretty early in the morning – are you awake at this hour to go and steal car parts?'

'I am finished for stealing car parts this morning,' he admitted. 'Come.' Igor swept his arm around Autumn's shoulders. 'Let's go.'

'Let's go,' said Robin, his hand guiding Mr Zaretsky's elbow. 'Your room is at the other end of the corridor.' The wandering resident let go of the fire-door handle and accompanied Robin. They shuffled through the nursing home together like an old married couple.

'Do you need a hand?' shouted Connie. She was in the middle of reviewing her nursing notes.

'No, I've got him.'

Robin helped Mr Zaretsky back into his bed. He covered his body with a comforter and made certain to raise the protective bedside railings. He also checked on the other residents. There were four men in the room and they were all sleeping soundly. Before leaving the room, Robin approached Mr Ramos in bed number two and rolled the sleeping resident onto his left side. Mr Ramos had to be turned every two hours in order to prevent pressure sores. Robin walked out from the room and closed the door. Connie was waiting for him at the nursing station.

'Is everything all right?'

'Yeah,' he said, 'everything's fine.' Robin sat down on a metal frame chair and took off his glasses. He rubbed his tired eyes. They felt like burned-out light bulbs in rusty sockets. 'How long have you worked here?' he asked.

Connie put down her notebook and tucked her hands into the pockets of her cardigan. 'Do you mean on the neuro-psychiatric floor?'

'Yes.'

'Five years.'

'What did you do before this?'

'I was a community service nurse in Trinidad.'

'Did you enjoy your work?'

'Yes, very much.'

'Did you work alone?'

'No, there were six of us. We would walk from our central health station to the different townships. When we arrived, the people would line up for us to check their blood pressure and sugar level. Along the way, depending on the season, we would find lovely sweet mangos and cashew fruits and avocados to eat.' Connie clapped her hands together and laughed. 'And we would gossip.'

'What brought you here?'

Connie stopped laughing. She quietly surveyed the fluorescent lighting, the uncomfortable chairs, the hard melamine surfaces. 'Opportunity.'

Robin put his glasses on and nodded.

'You've been here a year – are you happy?' she asked.

'No.'

'What did you do before this?'

'Before I was a health-care aide?'

'Yes.'

'I was in health care.'

'I'm surprised that you don't like your work. You seem to have a good understanding of the residents. In fact, the ones under your care seem to be improving.'

'For example?'

'Mr Zaretsky – he used to fall down all the time and now he's wandering the building without any assistance.'

'He was falling down because of a medication error.' Robin reached over to the medical records and withdrew a large plastic binder with 'Zaretsky' on the spine.

'What are you doing?'

'I'll show you,' he said.

'You can't look at the residents' medical records – they're confidential.'

'Here,' pointed Robin. He had opened the chart to the doctor's orders section. 'Dr Adler discontinued the Haldol about a month ago and switched him to Risperdal.'

Connie took the chart and examined the order.

'He was falling down because of the extrapyramidal side effects of the Haldol.'

'The what?'

'Mr Zaretsky has Parkinson's disease. The Haldol made his symptoms worse. If you look in the pharmaceutical compendium you'll see that Haldol is contraindicated in Parkinson's.'

'I think something is wrong here,' she said.

'What?'

'This isn't Dr Adler's handwriting.'

'Are you sure?'

'I've worked here long enough … '

Robin shrugged.

'Your other patient, Mr Ramos, how come he's so quiet all of a sudden?'

'I'm not sure what you mean. He's always been quiet. The last stroke left him aphasic.'

'I mean, why is he so different over the last week? He isn't fighting with the staff. He isn't crying. He suddenly seems to have settled in better.'

'Don't ask me.'

Connie reviewed the doctor's orders pages in the Ramos chart. She would occasionally look up from the chart and meet eyes with Robin. There had been no medication changes noted for several months.

'I'm going to finish my rounds.' Robin pushed himself out of the chair. As he walked toward the recreation area he glanced back at Connie. She had removed several of the medical folders from their shelves and stacked them in a pile. The charts belonged to Robin's section of the ward.

The recreation area was a large empty room surrounded by geriatric chairs. Robin walked across the room directly to the upright piano. He lifted its lid and put his hand inside the casing. The smell of woodworm killer wafted out from the inside of the instrument. His fingers searched the back frame ribs until he found the plastic bag. Robin removed the bag, closed the lid, placed the stolen bundle in his pocket, and left the room without a trace.

Kookla traced a leaf of lettuce across Luigi's nose. His chewing noises reminded her that Attila the goldfish also needed feeding. Kookla went to the aquarium and opened a plastic container. The fish food smelled like sea water and looked like pencil shavings. 'I can't stand Duffer,' she thought to herself. She milled the material between her thumb and index finger while Duffer watched. He sat on the hammock like a kid on a swing. Kookla peppered the top of the fish tank with the food and waited until Attila emerged from the hull of a sunken model ship. His kissing face gathered the sinking particles. 'There you go, fatty,' grinned Kookla. After sealing the container she sat back down on the floor.

Once, every so often, Kookla allowed herself the indulgence of a favourite little game. She would identify a target, draw a circle around it with her mind, and then remove its gravity. The object would suddenly hurtle skyward. When it struck the limits of the atmosphere it would shrink into nothing and finally disappear. A tiny white flare might appear for an instant. She focused this circle around her friend Duffer.

'Why are you smiling?' he asked.

'No reason.'

He stretched out on the hammock and waited. They hadn't spoken for an hour. Duffer brushed a foot against the floor and started the hammock rocking.

Kookla focused on Attila. He was drifting near the bottom of the tank behind a belching clam shell water filter. She had received the fish as a present from Duffer. That was six months ago, when she and Duffer had joined Autumn for supper.

Autumn had suggested a Chinese restaurant down the street from his studio. When they arrived at the restaurant a smiling hostess greeted them and led them to a table. Along the way they had to pass over a miniature bridge. Its columns were decorated with golden dragons and its canopy was hung with paper lanterns. Underneath the bridge was a penny-scattered fish pond. Kookla halted in the middle of the bridge and leaned over the railing. She stood there for a while watching the swimming goldfish.

At the end of the meal, while Autumn was disassembling his paper drink umbrella for the Chinese newspaper inside, Duffer called for the waiter. He whispered something into the waiter's ear. The waiter nodded, looked sideways at Kookla and then hurried off.

'What are you up to?' she asked.

'None of your business.'

A few minutes later the waiter returned and presented Kookla with a large bottle of Chinese cooking wine. Kookla stopped crunching the bits of her fortune cookie and stared at the waiter.

'What is this?'

'It's for you,' explained Duffer.

Kookla took the bottle.

'Oh my god!' she exclaimed. 'There's a goldfish inside!'

It took Autumn almost two weeks to find a decent-sized aquarium. In the meantime the goldfish, whom she had decided to name Attila, seemed perfectly happy inside his wine bottle. Kookla fed him a single pinch of fish food every day and delighted in his healthy growth. On the day of Attila's transfer to the fish tank, after the water had gushed out of the bottle, the goldfish got stuck. Attila was too big to slip through the neck of the decanter. The three of them stood there speechless. The poor fish, they realized, had gotten too fat.

Duffer reached for a mallet but Kookla slapped his hand away. She refused to consider this option. The same thing applied to not feeding the fish, shaking him out ketchup style and cracking the bottle with heating and chilling. Kookla and Duffer were out of ideas. Autumn ran into the kitchen. He returned with a crooked smile and a white plastic drinking straw. His intention was to increase the air pressure behind the fish.

Autumn reclined in the bathtub. He inserted the straw in the neck of the bottle and gave Kookla and Duffer a thumbs-up. Then, after a series of deep breaths, he tipped the bottle upside down and started blowing. Water poured onto his chest. The fish dropped down and plugged up the shoulders of the bottle. Autumn tried blowing harder. A pocket of air began to expand behind the fish. And slowly, very slowly, the fish began to enter the neck of the bottle. Kookla started clapping her hands. Autumn kept blowing until he nearly passed out. He finally gave up with a gasp.

'What happened?' she asked.

'I couldn't blow any harder.'

The problem, according to Autumn, involved the airway. The fish's body, as it entered the neck of the bottle, collapsed the plastic drinking straw and cut off the necessary air supply.

What they needed, he reasoned, was a method of generating continuous air pressure behind the fish. Autumn refilled the bottle with water and returned it to Kookla.

The three of them sat on the hardwood floor and listened to the bubbling of the empty aquarium. Kookla stared at the stranded fish. She then stared at Autumn. The front of his shirt was dripping wet and his pants were soaked. Kookla had an idea. She whispered something into Autumn's ear. He looked surprised, but he reached into his back pocket and produced a small shining square of foil. Kookla took the package, broke its seal and removed a condom. Duffer shook his head in dismay.

Kookla carefully unrolled the condom, then got a box of baking soda and a jug of white vinegar from the kitchen. She heaped some baking soda inside the condom and twisted it tight. Then she added, above the baking soda, a portion of vinegar. With the ingredients in place she knotted the condom, stuffed it inside the bottle and called out, 'Bombs away!' The depth charge sank to the bottom of the bottle. Attila floated above it. A few seconds later the twist in the condom unwound and the contents mixed. The resulting CO_2 gas quickly inflated the condom and displaced the water from underneath the fish. Water started to trickle from the bottle's mouth. The fish's helpless face and bulging eyes narrowed through the neck. Suddenly, Attila popped out of the bottle and landed on the floor. Kookla shrieked and rushed to scoop him up and drop him into the aquarium. The goldfish wasn't moving. She turned away and closed her eyes.

But Attila's gills and fins began to stream. 'I think he's moving,' said Duffer. The three of them watched as he eventually regained his bearings. At first he flitted back and forth against the glass, but soon he was he paddling around the aquarium like the Grand Marshall of the goldfish parade.

'Hello … hello … ' repeated Duffer. He was sitting on the hammock waiting for Kookla to respond. She just sat on the floor and stared at the goldfish. Duffer unbuttoned his overcoat. The studio was getting hot and he wanted to leave.

Kookla turned away from the goldfish. 'What do you want?'

'I want to find Robin.'

'Is that really what you want?'

'What do you mean?'

'I mean maybe you're here because you know that Robin is gone and Autumn is gone and you wanted to find me alone.'

Duffer was perspiring.

'Sit down beside me,' she said.

Duffer removed his overcoat. The sleeves fell from his arms like overcooked meat from a bone. He sat down beside Kookla.

'I know where to find Robin.'

'Tell me,' he said.

'First you need to convince me.'

'Convince you of what?'

'That you won't hurt Robin.'

Duffer abandoned the conversation. He reached for his overcoat as if it were a parachute. Kookla took hold of his wrist. 'Do you really want to help Robin?' she asked.

'I want to help Robin,' he said. 'What do I have to do to convince you?'

Kookla thought for a moment. 'Why don't we start with a bus ride?'

'The ride to the steam bath was not so bad,' said Igor. He was naked except for a white cotton towel around his shoulders and a pair of plastic sandals. 'Give me your clothes.' Autumn was sitting on a wooden bench with a towel around his waist. He handed Igor his clothing.

'Your car has no heat.'

Igor removed a disposable razor from his locker. He then stuffed Autumn's clothing into the narrow cubicle and forced the door closed. 'Don't you have to lock it?' asked Autumn.

'It is unnecessary,' Igor replied.

The steam bath was in the basement of an old utilities building. Members had to walk to the rear of the building, descend a flight of concrete steps and open a metal door. An attendant behind the door buzzed them in. He sat at a desk with a book, a portable heater and a large checkered thermos. Igor had explained to the attendant that Autumn was his guest. They argued in Latvian. The attendant crossed his arms and looked at his thermos. Igor put some money into the thermos.

As they walked from the change room to the showers they passed a number of different rooms. One contained a set of free weights and a medicine ball. This room was unoccupied. Another room contained a man with black goggles roasting under a sun lamp. The last room contained a group of several men, most of them naked, playing card games and backgammon and chess. They were sitting at fold-out tables and drinking hot tea from styrofoam cups. A grey-haired woman with a white apron circulated among them. She was carrying a tray of small glasses half-filled with a dark liquid.

'Is Melnais Balzams,' pointed Igor. Autumn didn't understand. 'Traditional Latvian alcohol, black medicine, made from bitter roots and herbs. The taste is very terrible – like pitch for mending tire.'

The shower facilities were very basic. The plumbing for the fixtures was exposed – galvanized steel with hot- and cold-water taps and lime buildup at the joints. Autumn lathered up with an industrial-smelling soap and rinsed off. During the shower he could see that Igor had thick, ropy scars on his ankles and knees and that his left hip was discoloured from a skin graft. Igor had always maintained that he was never at fault for the spectacular car accidents that caused them, and he insisted that if it weren't for his beautiful and temperamental vehicle he would be either dead or in a coma. He considered this a blood tie with his car and claimed that he would never drive another vehicle.

Autumn understood this tie and when, as a favour to Igor, he painted a sign on the front door of his garage, he combined Igor's face with the demolished body of the Mistress. The vehicle resembled Igor, held an ice pack to a throbbing red bump on its roof, and smoked a broken cigarette. Igor loved the painting so much he kissed Autumn on both cheeks after the unveiling.

After the shower they walked to the steam room. A fat man with a beard stepped in front of Igor. The man was rubbing the top of his bald head with a towel. He was naked except for a heavy gold watch on one wrist, a gold bracelet on the other, three gold chains with medallions around his neck, and at least three gold rings on each hand. He smiled at Igor with gold-capped teeth. Igor did not return the smile. He and the fat man started to quarrel. Their voices intensified as they moved in closer together. There was a great deal of gesturing and chest expanding. Suddenly the fat man reached down and feigned a grab at Igor's testicles. Igor laughed and drew back slightly. The fat man kissed his knuckles and uttered what must have been a threat. In response Igor raised his plastic razor and waved it in the man's direction. They parted on good terms.

'What was that all about?'

Igor opened the door to the steam room and ushered Autumn inside.

'That is Gregor,' he said. 'He is a car thief.'

The sauna was shaped like a rectangular theatre with three tiers of seating. The temperature inside was blistering hot and Autumn could feel his skin layers separate. A rumbling sound from the underground boilers, like the passage of a subway train, permeated the choking atmosphere. A red-skinned man reclined on the third tier. Igor greeted him with a 'sveiks.' The man nodded hello and slid over to one side. Igor sat down beside him and started inhaling and exhaling steadily through his mouth and nose. With his third respiration he started to cough. The coughing progressively worsened until Igor had to stand up, lean forward and clear his throat into his towel.

'Oh.' He sat down. 'The wet steam is very good.'

'This is unbearable,' said Autumn. He sat down on the first tier and scalded his ass on the tiles.

'Gregor is an excellent car thief.' Igor wiped the sweat from his face and his neck and started shaving. 'But I do not wish to work with him and that is why he is for grabbing my balls.'

'How do you know him?'

Igor tapped his razor on the edge of the tile bench. 'I know him from before. He purchased the crashed cars from my garage. He would switch the inspection numbers from a crashed car with a stolen car. This it would make the stolen car legitimate.'

'You were aware of this?'

'No.' Igor stopped shaving and rubbed a swollen ankle. 'I became suspicious later when he asked me to repair the strip-and-runs.'

'What's a strip-and-run?'

'It is when a thief strips a car of its valuables and leaves the stolen car for police to find. When police find car they make the chassis for an auction. The thief he buys the chassis, which is not so registered as stolen, and builds the car back together. It is very clever.' Igor massaged his sore ankle. 'Fuck it, this pain!' he said.

'What's the matter?'

'I am with these metal screws in my ankles. It is from the surgeries. If I am in the sauna for too long the metal gets burning.' Igor pointed at a metal bucket on the floor. 'Go please to make with the ice water from the faucet.'

Autumn crouched beside the faucet and turned the squeaking valve. 'Why don't you steal cars for Gregor?' he asked. A gush of icy water poured into the bucket.

'Please make it to the top,' he said.

Autumn passed the bucket up to Igor. He steadied the bucket by holding onto the rim with one hand in the water. His fingers felt like they were caught in a mousetrap. 'Be careful,' he said, 'it's biting cold.'

Igor dipped his hand into the bucket and wet his ankles. 'Ah,' he said, 'is much better.' He wet his knees and scooped a handful of the freezing water into his mouth. He then spat the cold water onto a metal wire hanging from the ceiling. The rumbling sounds in the sauna grew louder and steam billowed out from metal panels in the walls. The temperature in the room increased.

'What did you do?' asked Autumn.

Igor jerked a thumb at the dripping wire. 'Thermometer.'

'Are you crazy?' Autumn locked eyes with the red-skinned man who was contentedly wiping the sweat from his armpits with both hands. 'I can't stand this.' Autumn stood up to leave.

'You asked me a question.'

'What?'

'You asked me why I do not steal cars for Gregor.'

'Why don't you?'

'Because I am not car thief.'

'But you steal car parts.'

'This is different.'

'I don't see how.' Autumn sat down. He was feeling light-headed.

'How long have you been going out with Kookla?' Igor asked.

'What does that have to do with stealing?'

'How long?'

Autumn rested his head in his hands. 'A year … maybe more.'

'And Robin, her first boyfriend, do you know how long they were together?'

'I'm not sure.'

'Four years,' he said. 'He is with her much longer. Maybe there is only a part of Kookla belonging with you. For you to try and keep this, to keep it away from Robin, it is like stealing.'

'I'm not a thief.'

'Robin would disagree.'

'Robin's gone.'

'No, he is back, and he has visited me and is wanting to find Kookla. If he finds Kookla she will go with him unless you are there to be with her. I think she is safer with you. I would like that you and Kookla are back together.'

'I understand what you're getting at,' said Autumn. 'You're talking about commitment, the degree of commitment … '

'What is degree?'

'A degree is how much. It can be measured. It's like measuring a temperature.'

'What is your degree of commitment to Kookla?'

Autumn shook his head. 'I don't know.'

'It is like measuring a temperature you say?'

'Yes.'

'One's temperature can change.' Igor showered Autumn's body with the bucket of icy water.

'It's a water cure,' complained Duffer.

'What's a water cure?'

'This game of yours. People used to try and remedy their ailments by drinking too much water. It was also considered a method of torture.'

'Come on,' she said. 'It'll be fun.'

'Where did you learn about this bus ride thing?'

Kookla hesitated. 'I learned it in a group.'

'What kind of group?'

'Never mind – you just sit there and pretend.'

Duffer crossed his arms and stared at Kookla. 'Am I sitting on the bus now or what?'

'Not before you pay your fare.'

'Fine.' Duffer produced a make-believe ticket.

'That's not going to do.'

'Why not?'

'Because it isn't real.'

'If it's a pretend bus it should have a pretend fare.'

Kookla disagreed. 'You've got to invest something real.'

Duffer unfolded his wallet. 'I've only got a couple of fives.'

'One will be enough.' Kookla took the money and walked over to the fish tank. She folded the bill into a container labelled 'Bus Fare' and returned. 'I use the money to buy pet food,' she explained.

'That's nice,' he said. 'And what's your investment?'

Kookla hugged her knees against her chest. 'Let's find out.'

Duffer waited. 'Are we on the bus now?'

'Yes,' she answered.

'Oh,' he started. 'Well, then, it's nice to see you, Kookla.'

'Nice to see you, Duffer.'

He was lost for a topic of conversation. 'I've just finished a show … '

'Tell me about it.'

'Not much to tell – I worked hard and hit my beats, you know.'

Kookla nodded. 'What was your show about?'

'The story involved a woman who was lonely for her son. The son was always away on business. He never visited his mother; he just sent her postcards. The postcards were very important to the woman. The set designer decided to cover everything on the stage with postcards – the walls, the floors, even the furniture.'

'I suppose we find out later in the play that she was writing these postcards herself.'

'No, her son wrote the postcards, but the stamps were always local. Her son had never left the city.'

'Did you play the son?'

'I played the postman.'

'Is this how your relationship with the woman develops?'

'Yes, I read her the postcards.'

'It sounds sad.'

'It was a good show,' said Duffer.

Kookla scratched her forearm. 'Why didn't you invite me to the opening?'

Duffer wasn't prepared for this question. 'I think this is my stop.'

'No,' she insisted, 'please tell me.'

'All right,' he said. 'Because you lost interest in theatre.'

'That's not true.'

Duffer lifted an eyebrow.

Kookla withdrew from the exchange. She seemed to be searching for words. In her frustration she pulled on her fingers. 'Duffer,' she said, 'what do you see when you ride on the bus?'

'What do you mean?'

'I mean right this instant, on the bus, what is it you see?'

'I see some empty seats with newspapers, there's garbage on the floor, the driver is wearing a cap – the back of his neck could use a shave.'

'Where are you going?'

'I'm going home,' he said, 'home to sleep.'

'I see things differently,' she said. 'My bus is driving through the country. It's early summer. The windows are open and the air smells like rain. If you listen carefully you can hear the cicadas. The destination of my bus ride is my father's farm.'

Duffer softened his tone. 'When was the last time you visited your father?'

'I've never been back for a visit.' Kookla concentrated on the bus ride instead. 'It's the trip to the farm that interests me.

The travelling with a friend. Having a lunch on your lap. Things like that. This may sound funny, but if it weren't for you sitting beside me, I wouldn't be able to think about going back home.'

Duffer was surprised to hear this. He settled onto the floor somewhat closer to Kookla. 'What worries you about going home?'

Kookla lay on her side with her head gently resting on an outstretched arm. She didn't know how to answer the question. 'My parents had a dairy farm. Most of the farmers around us planted grains. We'd often see their hired hands collecting flats of hay into bushels.'

'Tell me about the landscape.'

'The landscape was beautiful. It was grassy and rolling with trees near the farmhouse. On the fields, in the early morning, the bushels would all steam from the damp.'

'What made the bushels steam?'

Kookla closed her eyes. She was remembering the meadows with the large grassy spindles. 'I think it's mildew,' she said. 'The mildew and the dampness together make the bushels hot. If they get hot enough they can catch fire.'

Duffer reached for Kookla's hand.

'I remember one rainy season when the crops on the neighbouring farms were destroyed. It was all on account of the mildew. There was a farmer near our property who, regardless of the crop damage, decided to bushel his harvest.' Kookla was quiet for a moment. 'Duffer,' she asked, 'have you ever read the story of the chimera?'

'No.' Duffer gently brought her hand toward his lips.

'It's a myth about a monster. The monster lived underneath a mountain. No one ever saw the monster, but the fire that it breathed could be seen between the stony cracks of the mountainside. There really is a place in Turkey called the Chimera. I read about it in a travel magazine. The face of the mountain is always dotted with blue flames. It's actually fountains of methane gas ignited by lightning. Ancient mariners used the Chimera as a landmark when navigating their ships at night.'

Kookla stopped herself and remembered the purpose of her story. 'One evening the farmer's bushels all caught on fire. All of the families in the area stood by and watched. I remember my father standing beside me. He rested a hand on my shoulder. It reminded me of the Chimera.'

Duffer kissed the centre of her palm.

Kookla yanked her hand away from Duffer, accidentally scratching his lip with a fingernail as she did. Duffer touched his tongue to his lip. It tasted salty and sharp. When he touched his shirt sleeve to his lip a drop of red blood quickly dried on the material.

'What's wrong with you?' he asked.

'What's wrong with *you*?' she shouted. Kookla stood up and walked away.

'It was just a kiss,' he explained. 'Just a kiss on your hand.'

She unlocked the studio door and left it open. Duffer sighed. He gathered up his overcoat and walked across the room.

'Close the door behind you,' she instructed.

'No problem,' he said. 'Like I told you before, this is my stop.'

'I doubt it,' she said. 'You're still acting like a passenger.'

Duffer took a moment and composed himself. He waited at the threshold. 'Before they disembarked, did Autumn and Robin behave like passengers?'

'No,' she said calmly, 'you're different.'

'And how's that?'

'Do you really want to hear this?'

'Yes, I want to hear this.'

'It's because you're always acting. It doesn't matter if you're on the stage or off. I'm sure you find it easier to relate to people when you're in character. A character that's like Duffer but rehearsed. I can't imagine that you experience anything directly. It's almost like you travel in between people, watching them through the window of a tour bus. That's why I call you a passenger.'

Duffer rested his back against the door. His hands were in tight fists under the crook of each arm. He spoke to Kookla very carefully.

'I think you've been riding along pretty good yourself,' he observed. 'There was musical study with Robin until he disappeared. Then, all of a sudden, when Autumn arrives, you assume a new interest in the fine arts … '

Kookla did not reply.

'Tell me this,' he asked. 'What will you do now that Autumn's gone?'

Kookla was furious. She pulled on the fingers of her right hand as if they were party crackers.

'Maybe you just need a lodestone,' he said. 'Do you know what that is?'

'No,' she replied.

'A lodestone's a magnet. Different kinds of animals have magnetic particles in their brains – it allows pigeons to fly home and lobsters to walk in single file on the ocean floor.'

'What the hell are you talking about, Duffer?'

'Humans also have this magnetic material in their brain. It's called magnetite and it allows for the perception of electrical fields. It basically helps us to find direction.'

'Are you saying that I'm lost without a boyfriend?'

'Not exactly.'

'I'm not lost,' she said, 'and neither Robin nor Autumn is my magnetic north, nor are you for that matter.'

'You're lying,' he said. 'You need somebody to accompany you, like I did with the bus ride, because you're afraid to travel alone.'

'Just go,' demanded Kookla. She gestured to the hallway.

Duffer closed the door to the studio. He felt ashamed for kissing Kookla and for his unexpected admission of jealousy.

He touched his aching lip. Kookla was right – she had warned him from the start that the bus ride would cost something real.

Reeling impressions of the sauna floor, getting carried, and being dressed roused Autumn. When he fully awakened he found himself buckled into the seat of a moving vehicle. He looked at the driver, who was smoking an unlit cigarette.

'Are you all right?' asked Igor.

'What happened?'

Igor smiled. 'If you are awake then I can smoke, yes?'

'Sure, go ahead.'

Igor pressed down on the car's cigarette lighter. A few seconds later it sprang up with a warm orange coil. He touched the glowing spiral to his cigarette tip. It burned red and a puff of white smoke left his nostrils.

'What time is it?' asked Autumn.

'The dashboard clock is not working,' Igor said. 'I think it is maybe from the time we left the prits four o'clock in the morning.' He replaced the car lighter.

Autumn touched his left eyebrow. It felt frozen. He gradually became aware of a dull ache in his sides.

'What happened?' he asked. 'And why are my ribs hurting so bad?'

Igor laughed quietly to himself. 'When you passed out from ice bath your head struck floor of steam room. It made me afraid because I thought you had stopped breathing. So I made CPR on you.'

'You made CPR on me?'

'I was pumping on your chest in way my Uncle Risha plays accordion.'

'Did you do mouth-to-mouth on me?'

Igor dusted the ash from his cigarette and nodded.

Autumn ran his tongue between his lips and teeth and tasted cigarettes.

'I don't mean to complain,' he said, 'but when do we get to your place?'

'It will not take so long.' Igor wiped the inside of the frozen windshield with his glove. The frost was on the outside. 'This reminds me of my family business.'

'What, the frost?'

'Yes … the clouding of the window. My family was famous for breeding sparrows.'

Autumn could not make the connection.

'In Latin the singing sparrow is called *passer*,' explained Igor. 'The bird of misfortune. For me and my family the sparrow it was good fortune. We bred beautiful European sparrows. Champion songbirds.' Igor rolled open his window and tossed out the cigarette. He cleared his throat and spat after it, then closed the window. 'When I was a boy I looked after the sparrows. It was my parents who taught the birds to sing. Singing for the sparrow, I learned, is to protect the territory.' Igor glanced over at Autumn. 'Did you know this about the sparrow?'

Autumn shook his head to say 'no,' which aggravated his headache.

'Our birds would sing continuously even if one should draw a curtain around the cage. Many of our sparrows, for this reason, were purchased abroad. I think so much of them were shipped to China.' Igor paused for a moment.

'What's wrong?' asked Autumn.

'The money from the sparrows afforded me admission to foreign universities. Before the universities I was to study in private schools. I am indebted to the birds.'

'So you grew up away from home?'

'Yes. My parents did not want me involved with the business with sparrows. Not until I was older.'

'Why do you say that?'

'Because of the clouding. The secret for making sparrows sing. After graduating from engineering I returned home. I travelled to Riga seaport on ship with name the Cassiopeia-Hamilton. A hired car it drove me to property. When I arrive at property I am startled by sound of the sparrows. The sparrows are singing so loud I have to run and search for parents with fingers in my ears. My parents were not in house so I went to look for them in ... how do you say in English, the birdhouse?'

'The aviary?' suggested Autumn.

'Yes, the aviary, but the aviary is empty except for birds. I am left to look in workshop. The workshop is forbidden to me. It is in workshop my parents train birds to sing. Because I am now older and returned from school, I enter workshop. The noise from inside workshop is incredible. It is brilliant and piercing and makes for a hole in the middle of sound. My parents do not hear me enter. They are sitting on edge of large wooden table and all around them are cages. From the floor to the ceiling are cages and inside cages maybe twenty or thirty sparrows. A few escaped sparrows are flying around room and colliding. There is horrible smell in room of burning. I watch my parents how they worked. They hold a sparrow in hand with glove, the glove is covered much with droppings, and in other hand is white stick. It is hot and with smoking red point. It is held an inch away from sparrow's eyes. I close the door and walk away from workshop.'

'A blinded sparrow has to sing in order to protect its territory.'

'Yes,' said Igor.

Autumn suddenly thought of Kookla.

The automobile decelerated along the curb. Igor coaxed the gears into park.

'Here we are,' he said. 'We are at my apartment.'

'What did your parents use to blind the sparrows?'

Igor pulled the parking brake and switched off the ignition. He sat there quietly in the driver's seat and regarded Autumn. 'Do you not understand?' he asked. Igor stabbed another cigarette between his lips.

Lips of the Floating White Lotus was Kookla's first choice of Indian teas. She put a teabag in her empty mug, then placed the kettle on the electric stove and wandered back to the comfortable chair. She sat down and felt her teeth chatter like a hurried stick along a picket fence. The studio was cold. She stood up and retrieved her favourite blanket, the one with the smiling cowboy and a friendly 'Howdy!' spelled out in his lariat. She inspected the empty bed.

Kookla drew the blanket around her shoulders. It was hard falling asleep without Autumn. She got up from the chair, switched off the studio lights and collapsed onto the bed. The evening before, she and Autumn had been under the covers together. She loved falling asleep with Autumn. He would snore and she would grind her teeth. On cold evenings like this one they would divide a pair of flannel pyjamas.

Kookla's thoughts were more approachable in the dark. She thought about Autumn and how he had left. There had been no drama to the situation. He had simply exited with the words 'I'd better get going.' It was an apology.

Duffer, more than likely, understood Autumn's motives. The two of them were reluctant friends. Kookla believed that their relationship was based on failings; Autumn lacked insight whereas Duffer lacked empathy. It was not unusual for one to make allowances for the other. This is how they came to know and eventually like each other.

As she drifted toward sleep, Kookla remembered back to the last time that she and Autumn and Duffer had been together. It was on a late-night bus back from a performance of *The Tempest*. Duffer had recommended the play. He had been a member of the cast until a complication developed that neither he nor the director could resolve. About halfway through rehearsals Duffer quit the company and another performer was auditioned.

The 'last call' bus was very crowded. Many of the passengers were disruptive and unbalanced. Fortunately, the three friends had arrived early enough to secure a set of three seats. They would have to travel for an hour on the bus in order to get back to their station.

'What did you think of the show?' asked Duffer. He had to raise his voice above the noise of the passengers.

'I liked it,' she said.

'The actors were excellent,' added Autumn.

Duffer nodded mopishly. 'Maybe I should have kept the role.'

The bus swerved between some potholes. Bottles and fast food containers tumbled underneath the seats. The occupants of the bus shouted and swivelled from their overhead handrails like hanging ballast. Kookla had to force a drunken man off her lap.

'This might be a stupid question,' ventured Autumn, 'but what was your role?'

Kookla punched Autumn's shoulder. Autumn rubbed his throbbing shoulder and mouthed, 'Ow!' She had specifically told him before the show not to ask Duffer about his replacement.

Duffer was distracted by the ruckus on the bus. 'What do you think was my role?'

Autumn guessed. 'Prospero?'

Duffer raised his voice. 'The director wanted me to play Miranda, the female lead.' Faces on the bus turned in their direction. 'He wanted to reproduce an authentic performance of Shakespeare, where all the characters are portrayed by male actors.

He was certain that I could play the female lead. I tried it for a while but it didn't work.'

'What was the problem?' asked Kookla.

'It was the company, the other actors – they were behaving like idiots. You know, making remarks about my sexual orientation.'

'What did they say?' asked Autumn.

'They called me a faggot and stuff like that.'

The rowdiness of the passengers diminished. Their attention suddenly shifted toward Duffer. Autumn and Kookla noticed a deep and pervasive quiet on the bus. Duffer was also aware of the silence but maintained a good volume.

'They never confronted me directly with the name-calling,' he said.

Kookla rested a calming hand on Duffer's shoulder but he withdrew. It was already too late. He was well into his act. The angry tone of his monologue increased. The physical gestures he used became broader. This was for the benefit of the bus-riding audience who sat in the far seats. His anger and how easily it attracted the curiosity of others frightened Kookla. Meanwhile, throughout Duffer's performance, Autumn simply sat quietly and stared out the window.

Kookla told Duffer to quit it, but the drunken crowd's attention spurred him on. He complained about the girlish queers who came onto him in acting class. Autumn just sat there gazing off into the distance.

'I told the director I wouldn't tolerate any rumours,' shouted Duffer.

Kookla reproached Autumn. 'Aren't you going to say something?'

Autumn continued to look out the window. His features were as neutral as a television test pattern. Then, all of a sudden, his expression changed. He seemed to take notice of something approaching the bus and quickly reached up for the cord.

There was a *ding* and the bus stopped. It was the only platform along the express route.

When the middle doors opened, Autumn stood up from his seat and pulled Duffer up with him. Kookla and all the other passengers watched as Autumn held on tightly to Duffer's lapels and kissed him. It was a long and passionate tongue-lolling Hollywood number. When they eventually separated Duffer was speechless. Every passenger on the coach was silent.

'I'll take my sister home and meet you later,' smiled Autumn. He teased Duffer's tresses. 'Be good.'

Kookla and Autumn descended the bus steps and the doors closed behind them. They tried not to laugh. The last thing they saw, as the bus pulled away, was Duffer's hand striking the exit door window.

Kookla opened her eyes. The digital clock was blinking 4:04 a.m. She covered her head with the blanket and half turned over on the mattress. The coolness of the cotton sheets eventually warmed to the temperature of her skin. She fell asleep. The kettle on the burner, however, was wide awake and whistling.

'Whistling and pissing are best done outdoors,' thought Duffer. With knees slightly bent he addressed the snowdrift at the entrance to Kookla's studio. His melody followed the looping hiss of each letter. D–U–F–F–E–R. At the end of his name he shook loose the last drops and did up his pants. The message steamed yellow in front of him. This seemed a more fitting way to say goodbye to Kookla.

As he walked away from the studio he was reminded of the stray cats that marked his mother's cottage for the consideration of a prissy calico named Tippy. The cottage was a two-storey structure in constant need of repair. Duffer's father had built it after the couple was married. It was the only thing that Duffer could associate with his father because after Duffer was born his father had never returned there.

The cottage was in a forested glen a good distance from the township. On weekday mornings Duffer walked a path to the roadway. A yellow school bus picked him up and drove him to school. There was no other opportunity for him to leave the property.

Duffer spent his time in class working on assignments. Teachers often complimented his abilities. He functioned well in groups and benefited from the company of other children. He couldn't make any close friends, however, because he had to take the bus home right after school.

Duffer's evenings consisted of suppertime with his mother and homework. He would later go upstairs to bed. His mother would allow him to read a comic book or two before she turned off the lights. Sometimes, late at night, an automobile would appear in the driveway. Duffer would sidle from his cot and hazard a peek through the curtains. He was familiar with five or six different cars that visited on a regular basis. By morning the car would be gone. Duffer's mother never mentioned any of the vehicles.

In early summer, when the weather became unbearably hot, Duffer's mother would refer to the time as the Season of the Toms because of the tomcats who pissed on the cottage stoop. Tippy would inhale their invitations every morning and meow in chorus with her suitors every evening. And Duffer would receive a kitchen-sink haircut – his mother cut his hair so short the kids at school made fun of his ears and scoured his scalp with their hands. Summer was usually a miserable time for Duffer. He would spend the whole two months alone with his mother at the cottage.

The year he was twelve, on the last day of school, the science teacher asked his pupils about their plans for the summer vacation. All of the children answered the question but Duffer. When the final bell sounded, the class dispersed screaming. The teacher stopped Duffer and asked him to stay for a moment. Duffer sat down on the front of his desk. His feet missed the floor by the length of a shoelace.

'Are you chewing gum in my class?' asked the teacher.

Duffer was startled. His mouth slowly opened. The flavourless gum sat on the point of his tongue. The teacher, who seemed insulted, crossed his arms and loomed closer.

'Give it here,' he instructed. Duffer spat out the gum and placed it onto his teacher's outstretched hand. Duffer had never really noticed his teacher's fingernails before – the right-hand fingernails were blackened and the left-hand ones were normal. The teacher examined the gum's moistness and elasticity, then stretched the gum between his thumb and index finger. His other hand reached into a pocket and pulled out a quarter, which he showed to Duffer, then he smeared the gum over top of it. The quarter was placed on the desk with the sticky side up. A small transistor radio, removed from a desk drawer, was then positioned beside it. The teacher attached the two objects with a set of copper wires. To Duffer's surprise, a musical crackle sounded over the radio speaker.

'Transistors require very little electricity,' he explained. 'The acid from your saliva in combination with the metals from the coin create a very weak battery. This small amount of power is just enough to make the radio operate.' Duffer was relieved by the demonstration. He was also very excited by the electronics. 'If you really have an interest in this stuff,' suggested the teacher, 'I could give you a special project for the summer.'

Duffer carried the heavy wooden box home on the bus and brought it into his room. He carefully lowered it onto the floor and opened it. The first thing he removed was a manual, then a silver cabinet and finally a variety of dusty components. He wiped the glassy pieces clean with a cotton handkerchief and sneezed.

He set the different parts on the floor in correspondence with a diagram from the operator's manual, then identified the individual pieces of equipment and began constructing the amateur radio.

The unit was in poor condition. Duffer had to replace a worn electrical cord with a double-outlet extension he borrowed from a vacuum cleaner. To complete the ground he had to attach one copper wire from the radio to the radiator and another to the window screen for the antenna.

The radio was an out-of-date communications training set, a 'Learn How To Build and Repair Radios at Home for Fun and Profit' order from the back of a matchbook cover. There was no protective housing to contain the apparatus. It was probably intended as a teaching model.

Duffer had the transceiver together in about five hours. Before he finally enabled the radio, he reviewed the procedures manual. At the back of it was an envelope that contained an old broadcasting licence.

Duffer studied the licence and prepared for a transmission. He put on the oversized headphones, adjusted the radio band to a low-frequency setting and switched on the unit. The vacuum tube filaments started to glimmer. A wonderful soda-pop static emerged as the coils gradually brightened. He triggered the microphone and repeated 'Delta … Foxtrot … Romeo … Delta … Foxtrot … Romeo,' the international telecommunications phonetics for his name. When there was no reply, he repeated his call sign and included the code letters 'QSL,' meaning 'Can you acknowledge receipt of my message?' There was still no reply. Duffer tried adjusting the frequencies. He repeated the sequence over and over until he finally noticed that his words were not even registering on the meter. His signal was not being broadcast.

He wrestled with the equipment for over two hours. The problem, he finally discovered, was a bulb as black as a rotten tooth. Duffer extracted it and referred to the manual.

This particular bulb, he read, was essential for the amplification of transmission signals. Duffer sat back on the footstool, discarded the headphones and turned off the radio. He looked out the window. The sky was beginning to darken at the edges. The radio, he realized, would only function as a receiver. This is why it had been donated to the school in the first place.

He kept the radio under his bed for a while, until the tedium of long summer days renewed his interest in it. He operated the radio at night, when the crickets transmitted their own signals. He had hoped to share in a conversation with an astronaut or listen to the emergency broadcasts of sinking ships. Instead, he picked up on local weather reports and redundant traffic chatter.

Duffer felt alone and the receiver only intensified his feeling of isolation. After a few more weeks of listening he decided to call it quits. Before signing off, he explored the more popular frequencies one last time. The messages were consistently dull, with damp signal strengths. Then, all of a sudden, Duffer encountered a strange turbulence, a repetitive rhythm which gradually quickened in its pace. He squeezed the headphones tight against his ears and leaned in toward the set. He carefully monitored the pulsing interference. It occurred on every channel on the AM and FM bands. Then, just as suddenly as it appeared, it disappeared. Duffer quickly scanned the bandwidths. He encountered normal transmissions with snow in the brackets. There was no trace of the desensing signal.

The signal was a communication of sorts, Duffer was convinced. Determining its source, however, was another matter. The only other person who knew about the radio was Duffer's science teacher, but he would be unable to broadcast a message so powerful as to affect every channel on the dial.

Duffer listened nightly for the interference. While waiting he studied the *Radio User's Manual*, searching for an explanation for the static. He read about the orbiting satellites carrying amateur radios, called OSCARS, that circled the planet. The OSCARS, however, could not account for the abnormal transmission. Duffer also read about the eleven-year sunspot cycle and its effect on signal propagation – signals reflecting off the solar-charged particles in the ionosphere could disappear for days at a time and then suddenly reappear with astonishing strength. But this hardly seemed like a reasonable explanation. Finally, an unexpected thought occurred to Duffer. Maybe the noise was a signal from God, a friendly reminder that Duffer was not alone in the world.

He kept listening. He would kneel at the foot of the night-stand every evening with the leather headphones strapped to his ears and his hands clasped together in prayer. He would stare at the equipment for hours. The voice of the receiver would whisper and crackle above him and the rows of radio tubes would flicker like candles heralding a breath of wind.

When the turbulence returned, he would close his eyes and listen. He could feel the signal's energy pouring through him like rain through a storm drain. It would gradually build and gush and then recede. Afterwards Duffer would turn off the radio and fall asleep, comforted by God's secret transmission.

By the end of the summer the signal had weakened. Duffer, however, was determined to maintain the communication. He struggled with adjustments to the equipment, disconnecting the audio filters and focusing the radio spectrum. Still, night after night, the impulse from God steadily decreased in volume. Duffer had an idea. He decided that an open wire antenna extending from the radio to a nearby tree would improve the reception. All he needed was a length of copper wire. He realized that the wire would have to be salvaged from somewhere in the house, preferably from an item that was rarely used. He took it from the doorbell.

The recovered wire increased the length of the antenna. Duffer's plan was to listen to the radio while setting up the new receiver – this would be the most efficient way of ensuring good reception. Later that evening Duffer climbed out of his bedroom window and onto the roof ledge. He sat there in his underpants and headphones, gently guiding a wire that extended from his bedroom to a nearby tree. He listened for the slightest variations in signal strength. There was still no discernible message. So Duffer waited. He would occasionally raise his hand with the wire and then drop it, trolling his ariel through the silent pools of radio waves in search of a nibble. His bare feet dangled just above the frame of his mother's bedroom window. A light from the window illuminated the tips of his toes.

Suddenly the static returned. Duffer held the wire in its current position and listened. The static throbbed slowly and gradually quickened. The light on his toes blinked in time with the static. Duffer looked down. There was a car in the driveway. He tipped his head underneath the roof ledge and looked inside his mother's bedroom.

There was a man in the bedroom. He was on his knees behind Duffer's mother, and he was naked except for a sweaty yellow undershirt. Duffer's mother was on her hands and knees on the mattress, her pillow covered with greasy cosmetic colours. With the man's every thrust the bed moved forward and back. Duffer could see that a leg of the bed galloped over a light plug. The light plug, with every shove, curved its two prongs in and out of a wall socket. The brutal scene flickered before Duffer's eyes with increasing clarity as the headphones conducted the disrupted electrical circuit.

Duffer stood in the snow outside Kookla's studio and stared at her window. He was angry with her. It was the same kind of anger and disappointment that he felt with his faith in the radio signal, but more than that, it was an anger with himself for believing that he was something special and for hoping that somebody important to him, like Kookla, would believe it, too. The light turned off in Kookla's studio. Duffer turned away from the urine-covered steps and walked back to his apartment. He would have to find Robin without Kookla's help.

'Help!' called a resident.

Robin stopped in the hallway. He ignored the resident and keyed in the combination to the nursing home's service door. He then entered a stairwell that led to a private staff room. The room was dark. It had a fridge, a candy machine, a rack of coats and a couch. A custodian was sleeping on the couch. Robin tried to find his coat.

'You're leaving early,' said the custodian.

'Did I wake you?'

The custodian checked his watch. 'Naw,' he said, 'it's almost five in the morning. I gotta get up and mop the dining room floor.' He stood up from the couch and arched his back. 'Hit the lights, wouldya?'

Robin switched on the lights.

'You need the time clock?' He squinted.

'No,' replied Robin. 'I'm not coming back.'

The custodian rubbed the back of his neck with a calloused hand. 'Good for you,' he said and left the room.

Robin found his coat and put it on. Before leaving he sat down on the couch, pulled up his socks and straightened his pant legs over his boots. It was cold outside. The buses wouldn't run for another hour, so he would have to walk to Kookla's studio. Robin settled back into the couch. It was going to be a long walk; just thinking about it made him feel sleepy.

The sleeping custodian reminded Robin of Duffer's frequent unexpected visits. When they were both students almost four years ago, Duffer would turn up late at night after losing his dormitory key. There was always an elaborate and entertaining explanation, like the one about the private party in a tattoo parlour where he had barely escaped with his skin. By the end of the story Duffer would be asleep on Robin's couch in the shape of an S, his shoes on the floor and his stockinged feet sticking out from under a blanket.

Robin remembered back to when he and Duffer first met. Duffer had been the victim of a hit-and-run accident. He was limping and confused, the right side of his forehead was bloodied, and when he tried to carry weight on his right leg he would fall to the ground. Robin rushed over and tried to support him.

'What are you doing?' asked Duffer. He tried to push Robin away.

'You've been injured.'

'Leave me alone.' Duffer wiped a smear of red blood from his face and looked at his watch. 'I've got an appointment …' He took a few steps away from Robin and fell to the ground.

'Stay right where you are.' Robin tried to examine him. Duffer's right eye was swollen and his eyebrows were crusted with dirt and blood.

'Make sure the coffee lid is on really tight this time,' Duffer said.

'What are you talking about?'

Duffer tried to sit up. Robin grabbed him by the shoulders and forced him back to the ground. He searched for assistance. Duffer resisted and Robin shouted, 'Stop struggling – you're in shock. Tell me, what's your name?'

'Duffer,' he said. His hand waved in the air as if he were hailing a cab. 'I've got to go …'

Robin gently pulled the waving hand back down along Duffer's side. He then tried to resume his examination. 'Duffer,' he said, speaking calmly, 'I'm just going to check and make sure that nothing's broken.'

Robin made certain that Duffer's airway was clear, then checked the pulses at his neck, wrists and ankles. Duffer had good circulation to his extremities. Next, Robin prodded gently at his abdomen, paying careful attention to the kidneys and spleen.

Finally, Robin examined Duffer's body for evidence of fractures. He started with the skull, which showed no sign of a compression fracture, and then worked his way down to Duffer's feet. Duffer yelled when his right tibia was touched. Robin lifted his pant leg and saw that his calf was covered in blood.

'I think you've got an open fracture.' He took off his belt and used it to splint Duffer's legs together.

'What are you doing?' he complained.

'This will stabilize your fracture.'

A man holding a newspaper suddenly appeared on the scene. He quietly watched as Robin held Duffer's neck in a fixed position. The man started to walk away.

'Hey!' shouted Robin. The man stopped. 'Can you call for an ambulance? This guy's been hit by a car – I think he's in shock and he's got a broken leg!'

The man looked at Robin, then announced 'Time' and placed his newspaper down on a metal desktop. A woman sitting behind the desk glanced up at the wall clock and repeated the word 'Time.' She made a short note in her examiner's notebook and then gestured for Robin to approach the desk. Robin sighed heavily and stood up from the floor. The standardized patient removed the belt from around his legs and whispered to Robin, 'You did fine.' He handed Robin the belt.

'No talking,' said the first examiner.

Robin leaned over the metal desk and looked at the piece of paper. It was marked 'Station 10.'

'Sign here,' indicated the examiner with her finger on the paper. She handed Robin a black plastic pen. He signed his name along a straight line at the top of the page. His signature balanced there as if it were on a tightrope. Robin returned the pen. The woman told him to move in closer. She held onto his identification and inspected the photograph, compared the signature, noted his student number and finally let go of the badge.

Robin, the standardized patient and the two medical examiners waited for the bell. Robin wiped his glasses with his shirt. The demands of the station had steamed up his lenses. When the final bell sounded, Robin was instructed to leave the room.

The examination was known as a bell-ringer; there were ten different doors and behind every door was a different problem. A note on the door provided a brief introduction to the station. The last one simply read 'Accident Victim.' The student would enter the room on the first bell, complete the assignment, exit the room on the second bell, and then walk over to the next station. This sequence was repeated ten times with ten students standing in front of ten doors.

Robin avoided the loitering medical students, particularly those who had gathered in excited or defeated circles. The examination was over and all that he wanted to do was relax. He had exhausted himself with one and a half months of continuous late-night studying – the kind of study where by two in the morning his brain cells were sizzling and his eyeballs were filled up with smoke. After the exam he decided to visit the university pub. A pull of cold draught would help extinguish any smouldering study-conscious nerve centres.

It turned out to be a typical Friday afternoon at the pub – the place was crowded and smoky and loud with music and people laughing. Robin pushed his way between the dart-throwing couples and approached the bar. He shouted for the bartender, pointed at a beer, paid for his pint, and then walked with his beer above his head through the jostling crowd. He made his way over toward a sitting area, which was just as crowded. There was one seat available on the couch. Robin poured himself onto it and spread out like warm pancake batter. He sat there beside another beer-drinking student, admiring the crowd and balancing the pint on his lap.

'It just occurred to me that everyone at the university must have finished their exams today,' he said to the student.

'What?'

Robin faced the student and raised his voice. 'Everybody's finished exams – that's why it's so busy in here.'

The other student shrugged politely and said, 'I wouldn't know.' He took a drink from his own pint.

Robin looked closely at the student. He looked somehow familiar.

'Where do I know you from?' he asked.

The student smiled and toasted Robin. 'Don't you remember? You just saved my life.'

'What?'

The student took another swallow from his pint and wiped the foam off his lip. 'Station 10.'

'Oh yeah,' recalled Robin. 'I didn't recognize you without the swollen eye and the broken leg.'

'What's your name?' Duffer extended a hand.

'Robin.' They shook hands.

'You did fine today, Robin.'

'Thanks. I think yours was the most difficult station.'

'You're telling me. You were my one hundredth performance of Accident Victim.'

'Do you know what the other nine stations were testing?'

'No, the standardized patients aren't allowed that kind of information.'

Robin counted on the fingers of one hand. The other hand was busy supporting the pint of beer. 'I think it went like this: meningitis, spousal abuse, myocardial infarction, traveller's diarrhea, spinal stenosis, suicidal ideation, genital herpes in pregnancy, ketoacidosis, unexplained weight loss and accident victim.'

Duffer's eyebrows seesawed. 'Why would they choose those topics?'

'Who knows? They could have chosen from any topic in all of medicine. The funny thing is,' confided Robin, 'they always repeat at least six of the ten stations every year.'

'How do you know that?'

'I've spoken with several graduates from the medical program. They told me about the stations on their exams.'

'Isn't that cheating?' asked Duffer.

'I don't think so. You never know – the format could have changed, and you still have to be prepared for the other four topics. It doesn't really change the amount of material that you need to study.'

Duffer took a drink. 'What area of medicine are you entering?'

'Neurosurgery.'

Duffer's eyebrows levelled. He gazed into his pint of beer. 'How long is that going to take you?'

'At least five more years,' said Robin. 'It could take seven or eight years if I subspecialize.' A quietness settled between them. 'And how about you? What kind of work do you do when you're not a standardized patient?'

'I'm an actor.'

'I'm sorry,' he said. 'That was a stupid question.'

'Don't worry about it. I do other things but that's my major interest. How about you? Do you have any interests other than medicine?'

'My background is actually in music. I've been studying classical piano since I was about five years old.'

'Did you ever perform?'

'I competed … '

'Are you still practicing?'

'Medicine takes up too much of my time.'

Duffer reached into his pant pocket and removed a crumpled piece of paper. He handed it to Robin. 'Here,' he said, 'read this.'

'What is it?'

'Read it.'

'It's an invitation,' Robin said.

'Yes.'

'It's an invitation for two people to one of your performances.'

'Yes.'

'When is it?'

'Tonight.'

'Tonight,' wavered Robin. 'I don't know. My head feels like a termite nest.

'Look,' Duffer argued, 'I've just recovered from a terrible accident.'

'Hold on a minute – it says here on your invitation that your stage manager is Kookla.'

'That's right. Do you know her?'

'Do I know her? Kookla's my girlfriend!'

'What do you mean?'

'Actually, we've just started going out – I'm not sure if we're boyfriend and girlfriend yet.'

'I can't believe that you're Kookla's boyfriend,' said Duffer. 'I knew that she was going out with someone. She told me it was someone she had met in a hospital. But it had never occurred to me that it might be one of the doctors. I figured that it might be one of the other … ' Duffer suddenly brought the glass of beer to his lips and took a drink.

'What were you about to say?' asked Robin. He raised his voice above the noise in the pub.

'Are you sure that Kookla never mentioned our perform-ance?' He pointed at the invitation. He was careful not to look at Robin.

'No,' he said. 'She never mentioned it.'

'She must be nervous. I'm nervous, too. This will be our first performance together.' Duffer drummed his fingers on his glass. 'I'm surprised that she never mentioned me.'

'Maybe she did and I just can't remember. Anyhow,' he raised his glass, 'break a leg.'

Robin and Duffer touched glasses. They tilted their heads back and finished their drinks.

Robin took a last look at the staff room. He thought about all his years of medical training. Now, here he was, a health-care aide, cleaning up after seniors in a government-subsidized nursing home. And it was Duffer who had put him here. Robin understood that he had done it to protect Kookla and harboured no resentment toward him. Duffer knew this, too. What Duffer didn't know was that Robin had continued his studies outside of school and that, because he loved Kookla, he was prepared to do whatever was necessary to make her better.

II

'Better … ' said Autumn. 'But I still need more blanket.'

Igor cast off his covers. 'Please to be quiet and go to sleep.'

Autumn resigned himself to his sagging portion of the pull-out mattress. Sharing the sofa bed was Igor's idea. Autumn lay on his back, then tried rolling over onto his side. With every small movement Igor bucked up and down beside him as if they were in a boat. Autumn attempted several positions before he was able to settle. Lying on his side, he noticed a skin-coloured circle on Igor's shoulder. Autumn poked at it with his index finger. It was a rubbery strip of pink adhesive.

'What are you doing?' snapped Igor. When he turned around to face Autumn the mattress surged upwards with an angry wave.

'What is that?' asked Autumn.

'It's a nicotine patch.' He turned away from Autumn and pulled an extra inch of blanket toward him. 'It's because I am not wanting to set you on fire.'

Autumn ran a hand along the perimeter of his mattress edge. He could feel the crusty burn holes in the material. He suddenly sat upright. The bed sloped toward him.

'You know what?' he said. 'I want to see Kookla.'

'That's good,' mumbled Igor. 'She is your Perespella.'

'Perespella,' he repeated. 'That's her gas station nickname. She told me that you said it means rotten fruit?'

Igor's face tightened. He then started laughing. 'In my language,' he chuckled, 'the word it means for one who ripens early. It is fruit on branch that is mature before others. It is a compliment.'

'You mean a windfall,' said Autumn.

'Yes … a windfall. Some people drop from tree. Others waste on bough. It is depending, like you say, on the wind.'

'I think you know Kookla much better than I do.'

'I am knowing her for much longer. When I first open garage seven years ago she is asking for job. She is not looking well. She has dirty hair and hungry face. I make her to work in the gas station office. At first she is to answer the telephone.' He thought for a moment. 'And to make poisonous coffee. Then one day, when I am without mechanic, I tell her to find me replacement. He must be to help me unplug many oil pans.'

'Did she find you a mechanic?'

'She does not call for mechanic. Instead she leaves office and enters garage and unplugs the oil pans.'

'Where did she learn this?'

'On her parents' farm. When she helped her father to repair his tractor and other equipment. She told me she hated office – it was stupid and boring and she wanted to work in garage. She must also to be paid more money. Fine. The next day she comes to garage in man's blue dungarees. They are trimmed at the cuffs and with black leather belt on her waist to prevent trousers from dragging.'

'That's how you met Kookla?'

'Kookla is fine mechanic,' he said. 'She is working very hard with good common sense. Of course she is to making me crazy. After work, for example, she is to only wash grease from hands with fresh lemons.' Igor stopped for a moment and laughed. 'I remember this picture very well. Kookla will not use spirit oil, only lemons – there are many of these buckets of lemons in garage. On busy day she was to leave many black lemon rinds clogging my sinks.' Igor shook his head. 'It did not matter because, for me, she is the most important in making it clear the practical aspects of mechanics. Kookla is happy with her work. When she is joining garage I am learning from her again to enjoy the pleasure of working with machinery.'

'But you have a doctorate in mechanical engineering – you were a professor and a researcher.'

'No matter,' said Igor. 'I am still for studying engineering. I am not religious but I think it is for me something spiritual.'

'What, mechanics?'

'Yes, it goes back to my childhood in Riga. Back to my Jewish upbringing in orthodox house. My family celebrated Sabbath night with candles and prayers and song. This was happy time for us. The passing of the Sabbath, however, it was a sadness. That is why my family kept a besamim.'

'What's a besamim?'

'It is a spice box. The scent of the spices is to make sweet the sadness of passing Sabbath. They are precious containers, made from silver and gold with likeness to synagogues and animals from forest. But my family's besamim is from Industrial Revolution, more modern, with filigree cylinder, piston wheels, smokestacks and steam domes. It is to resemble a steam locomotive. I remember the smokestacks make a scent from warm cinnamon. Later, when family is wealthy from trading with East, foreign spices like ginger and cherry blossom are to stoke little engine.'

'You attribute a great deal of importance to this spice box.'

'Yes, it is religious association, and it is beautiful machine and sensual fragrances. I am still observing my fascination with this engine.'

The conversation was making Autumn sleepy. He decided it would be better to contact Kookla in the morning when he was properly rested. He tucked his hands behind his head and sank into the mattress. 'This is all very interesting,' he yawned.

'Before you fall asleep,' prodded Igor, 'I have one last thing to tell you.'

'What's that?'

'The locomotive,' he said. 'It is also of significance for Kookla. Her dungarees, the ones I had described to you, they were old, and they had the emblem of a railroad on the breast pocket.'

'Maybe she got them at a second-hand store?'

'No, it does not make sense that she will buy a pair that are so large. I think they are taken from a railroad station.'

'If you feel such a strong connection with Kookla,' asked Autumn, 'why would she quit your garage?'

'Because of something that happened to me from Robin.'

'What happened?'

Igor reached down to the clothes on the floor. He stirred through the pile and uncovered a grey lighter. He snapped open the lid and drew back on the striker.

'You must promise me to never repeat this to Kookla,' he said.

'I promise,' said Autumn.

The lighter's dry wick caught on fire. Igor held the brown flame underneath his left arm. 'You will have to remove it for me,' he told Autumn.

'Remove what?'

'I am showing it to you,' he said tersely. 'The skin patch.'

A patch of dark smoke was skimmed from the air with a water-soaked towel. Kookla was marching through the studio with the towel waving around her like the tail of a Chinese dragon. She was still half asleep. The Emergency Operator part of her brain, the part that delivers simple instructions in a clear and friendly voice, had her awake enough to perform the necessary tasks. She had turned off the electric stove, removed the blackened kettle from the element, and opened a window. Once the smoke in the studio cleared she sat down on the bed. The clock was lying sideways on the floor – it read 4:34 a.m. The room smelled like burned metal and was getting colder because of the open window. Kookla could not believe that she had slept through a full kettle of whistling hot water. She stared at the charred kettle.

Her last careless fire had occurred years ago during an overnight shift at the garage. She was in the middle of a transmission job when Igor started calling. When Kookla found him he was dancing in the storage room doorway. It was the most ridiculous thing that she had ever seen and it made her laugh and clap her hands. Then Igor turned around and she could see that his pant leg was on fire. He was shouting in Latvian and trying desperately to undo his trousers. Kookla ran into the gas station office and grabbed the chemical extinguisher attached to the wall. She returned and coated Igor's hair, his eyebrows and the burned skin on his leg with a spray of chalky powder.

'What happened here?'

Igor shook his head and blinked his eyes.

Kookla noticed a soggy cigarette filter hanging from Igor's open mouth. It was also covered with the fine chemical powder. She plucked the butt from his lips and threw it on the floor. 'Let's go,' she said.

Kookla drove Igor to the hospital. She parked the truck outside the Emergency department and carefully helped Igor down from his seat. They walked together, like a three-legged man, to the fluorescent admissions desk. At two in the morning the place was deserted. The triage nurse who worked at the desk charted Igor's name and a few of the details, then another nurse appeared and led them into a small procedures room.

The procedures room was illuminated by an overhead surgical light. It contained several white medical cabinets along the walls, a surgical table and two stools. A single white sheet of waxy paper was draped over the table's three segments: head, trunk and legs. Kookla sat down on the rolling stool. Igor climbed onto the table with some difficulty. The pain from his leg was increasing. A stand near the table held a kit sealed in plastic; it was labelled 'Suture Tray.' The surgical setting made Igor queasy.

'The doctor will be with you soon,' said the nurse. She left them alone in the room. About ten minutes later a young doctor arrived. The room's sterile brightness caused him to wince. He was wearing a pair of hospital greens and a lab coat. Kookla noticed that the hair on one side of the doctor's head was pressed flat. He must have been awakened from a nap.

'Good morning,' he said. He glanced over at Igor. 'I see you have a burn that needs dressing.' He lay down a clipboard and walked over to the room's basin. He pumped his foot on a floor pedal and started the water gushing. A squirt of pink cleanser dropped onto his palm. While he was busy washing, Kookla explained what had happened. The doctor, who seemed to be listening, or maybe just waking up, removed his foot from the pedal and dried his hands. He sat down on a second stool near the table. Kookla quietly rolled her stool over toward the doctor so that they were sitting on either side of Igor. They were close enough that Kookla could discern an early facial stubble and a scent that combined soap, sleep and coffee.

The doctor unwrapped a pair of white latex gloves and pulled them on. He quietly hummed to himself as he examined Igor's leg. The tune was oddly comforting.

'What's that song?' asked Kookla.

'It's "Love for Three Oranges,"' said the doctor. He trimmed off an edge of burned trouser with curved scissors. 'It's by Prokofiev. I'm learning the opening phrases on piano.'

The doctor set aside the scissors and completed his assessment. 'This is a second-degree burn with edema and blistering,' he told them as he picked up a scalpel. 'You won't need admission to the hospital but you'll need a debridement. A few of these blisters have already ruptured.' He gestured toward the peeling skin with the blade of the scalpel. 'It will be better for you if I remove the debris before it gets infected.' The doctor put down the scalpel and tugged off the dirty gloves with a snap. He then stood up and tossed the inside-out gloves into a garbage pail. 'Before we begin you'll need some vigorous rinsing with sterile water, the colder the better, and maybe a tetanus shot. Do you remember the last time that you had a booster?'

'I cannot say for certain … ' lamented Igor. 'Perhaps in my chart?'

'Have you ever been here before?' asked the doctor.

'Many times … '

Kookla nodded her head in agreement.

'No problem.' He scribbled something on the clipboard. 'One other thing,' he said. 'This is going to be painful.' He looked up from the clipboard and met Igor's eyes. 'You're going to need a strong analgesic.'

'A strong anal what?' exclaimed Igor. He sat up on the table, his eyes round as hubcaps.

'Igor,' calmed Kookla, 'analgesic … pain medicine.' She smirked quietly at the doctor.

'Oh,' relaxed Igor. 'That would be good.'

The doctor completed his note. 'I'm going to leave these orders for the nurse and she'll come in and prepare you. The minute that you feel comfortable we'll start the debridement. I'll also find out about your tetanus status. Don't worry,' he promised as he walked from the room, 'we'll get you fixed up in no time.'

Kookla followed the doctor from the room. 'Is he going to be okay?' she asked.

'Your friend will be fine.'

'Should I stay with him?'

'Well,' thought the doctor, 'he's going to be out of it with the pain medicine.'

'Perhaps I should wait for him elsewhere?'

The doctor looked up at a wall clock. It read 2:45 a.m. He gently nudged his glasses back into place. 'You're welcome to relax in the waiting room,' he offered. 'The maintenance staff won't be around for another hour.'

Kookla made a quick assessment of the hard plastic seats. The doctor made another suggestion. 'Then again, we could go visit the medical records.'

'You need to get Igor's old chart?'

'That's right.'

Kookla considered the invitation. While she was thinking, the doctor stepped lightly behind her. He seemed to be preoccupied with the ceiling. 'Don't move,' he instructed. 'Just reach behind with your hands.' Kookla wasn't sure what he was doing but she complied. The doctor slipped out of his lab coat and placed it onto her shoulders. 'I don't want Security bothering us,' he whispered. He motioned upwards to a ceiling-mounted video camera.

The white cotton lab coat was surprisingly heavy. Its side pockets were bulging, one with books and the other with instruments. Kookla discovered a simple grey tuning fork in the instrument pocket. She held it up to the light and examined its stem. It was engraved.

'Is your name Robin?' she asked.

'Yes. Yours?'

She tapped the instrument once on her wrist. It shivered and whispered a *w* sound. Before the tone faded she smiled at Robin and held the tuning fork up to his ear. He leaned forward and listened. The resonance ended.

'My name is Kookla.'

'Kookla,' he said, 'the medical records are over this way.' They followed a service route marked 'Hospital Staff Only.' The hallway was dark and Kookla stayed close to Robin. They pushed through a series of wire-glass swing doors. The hospital corridors narrowed beyond every doorway and the distance between doorways kept increasing.

'It isn't much further,' encouraged Robin. He stopped for a moment and disappeared into a dark and recessed corner of the hallway. When he returned he presented Kookla with a handful of crackers. 'Supper tray shelving,' he said. 'Help yourself.' Kookla nibbled on the crackers while Robin disclosed a few of the hospital's secrets. She learned that Robin was not the staff person on call but the resident student doctor. The 'Staffman' was asleep in his office. He was to be awakened only for a real emergency. Robin also explained the special colour codes that were used over the hospital speaker system. For example, a code blue meant a cardiac arrest, a code white meant a violent patient, and a code black meant a bomb threat. There was also the transfer of dead patients. Robin explained that some of the hospital gurneys have a hidden bottom where a body can be concealed. If one of these gurneys is unavailable the patient is sometimes transported, seemingly asleep, in a wheelchair. They turned a corner and arrived at the medical records.

'Would you like to see the display cabinets?' Robin asked.

'What's inside them?'

'Curiosities, antiquated surgical instruments, the disease of the week, artificial limbs … '

'No thank you,' Kookla replied, 'it sounds way too creepy.'

'There is one exhibit you might find interesting. I can show it to you later.'

They entered the medical records and searched for Igor's identification number. The room was a network of narrow intersecting aisles, the walls of each aisle consisting of multiple tiers of crowded medical filing. It was musty and complicated. While searching for the chart Kookla became more talkative. She was enjoying herself despite the difficulty in locating Igor's records.

'How are we expected to find this thing?' she asked.

'Concentrate on the catalogue numbers,' advised Robin. 'It's impossible otherwise.'

Kookla climbed onto a rolling stepladder and reached for the upper-level files. Robin wheeled the stepladder back and forth according to Kookla's instructions. He was enjoying himself as well.

'I found it!' she hollered.

'Keep it down,' cautioned Robin. 'You're not supposed to be in here.'

Kookla glided down the stepladder and landed on the floor with an *oomph*. She had forgotten about the extra weight in the lab coat pockets. Robin took the file and made a quick review of Igor's immunization status.

'Your friend's up to date with his shots,' he said. 'We had better head back to the Emergency.'

'Not before we visit that display cabinet you mentioned.'

Robin guided Kookla through a section of the original hospital. He told her the wing was more than a hundred years old. The corridors were even narrower than before and the ceilings were higher and vaulted like the inside of a church. There were very few windows. The floor tiles were made from small black and white ceramic hexagons fit into precise geometric patterns. Kookla noticed that a series of copper filaments accompanied the baseboards on either side of the hallway. These copper tubings glided up along the frames of every door and were welded shut at waist level. Robin gestured at the doorway lintels. Above them were tiny cups of glass held in place with tarnished metal fittings. These fixtures, Kookla learned, represented the hospital's early coal gas lighting system.

'Here we are,' announced Robin. They stood before an elaborate and enormous wall-mounted wooden frame. Behind the heavy casement glass, pinned onto a background of velvet, were hundreds and hundreds of individual objects. Each object had pinned underneath it a rectangular piece of paper with the object's display number.

'What is this?' asked Kookla.

'Look closer.'

Kookla examined the objects more carefully. There were peanuts and small coins and shirt buttons. She squinted at Robin.

'Is this the display case you were talking about?'

'This display,' he began, 'is the Museum of Aspiration. Everything you see in here is a foreign body removed from the lung of a child.'

'Oh my god,' gasped Kookla.

'The object is removed with a bronchoscope after a chest X-ray determines its location. This collection probably accounts for more than fifty years' worth of aspirations. Most of the objects are junk, I admit, but if you take the time … '

'I see a tooth,' interrupted Kookla, 'and over here's a safety pin.' Her eyes skipped over the various levels of shapes and textures. Finally, near the bottom, she stopped.

'What is this?'

Robin crouched down beside Kookla. Their shoulders brushed. 'It looks like a sailing ship.'

'I think you're right,' she said. 'It must be made from gold. I think it's a charm from a charm bracelet.'

'I would give you this sailing ship as a present,' he said, 'if I could.'

Kookla was surprised by Robin's admission. She straightened up and placed a hand on the cabinet. 'You would have to break into the display,' she grinned. 'It wouldn't be easy. This case is well made. And I'm sure that any meddling would shatter the glass.'

'You're probably right.'

They stood together awkwardly for a moment.

Suddenly Robin's pager started beeping. He unclipped it from his jersey and looked at the message. 'Oh shit,' he exclaimed, 'it's Emergency.' They hurried back to the procedure room where they ran into the admissions nurse.

'Where have you been?' she asked. 'And why is she wearing a lab coat?'

'Never mind,' answered Robin. 'What's going on?'

'Your burn patient is discharged.'

'Come again?'

'The Staffman completed the debridement.'

'When?'

'Shortly after you left. He woke up for his rounds and inspected the Emergency. That's when he found the department unattended and your patient fully prepped. Anyhow, the patient is cleaned and dressed and ready to go.'

'I was busy in medical records.'

'Tell it to the Staffman,' she said. 'He's waiting for you in the office.' The nurse turned and walked away. Kookla handed the lab coat back to Robin.

'Don't look so worried,' he told her. 'This is just a rotation. I'm not applying for work in the Emergency.'

Kookla touched his forearm. 'Goodbye, and thank you,' she said. Robin nodded graciously.

A month later Igor was back at work, happily repairing vehicles and smoking his cigarettes near the fuel lines. Kookla, however, was distracted by thoughts of Robin. Unfortunately, his telephone number wasn't listed, and the hospital wasn't helpful. And Robin knew her only by her first name. Kookla considered a trip to the hospital, but she had no idea when Robin would be there. He was probably positioned in a different department. He might even be in a different hospital.

Kookla felt disheartened. She tried to focus on her work at the garage. Igor allowed her the distance. He was convinced that she was still angry with him for resuming smoking.

Then, one afternoon, Kookla found something attached to her locker. It was a large paper envelope, faded and held together with curling bits of tape. On the envelope was written 'To Kookla, care of Igor.' She tore it open. It contained a single sheet of black film. Kookla held it up against a window. The greyish picture on it resembled two surging crescents of water divided by a tributary. She was holding a chest X-ray, and in the right lung was the contour of a white sailing ship run aground on an airway. The old radiograph was, in itself, quite precious. But the real gift, she understood, was Robin's success in locating the film. It had taken a month's worth of searching. That he had somehow accomplished this without the person's name or filing number was incredible. Finding Kookla was another matter. He must have reviewed the hospital admission information that Igor provided. Kookla flipped over the torn paper envelope. On its reverse was Robin's telephone number.

The studio was finally clear of its smoke, but the cold air inside left a metal taste in her mouth. Kookla walked over to the sink and tossed in the dampened towel. She then sat down on a steamer trunk and brushed a strand of hair from her face. Her hair smelled like campfire. Kookla stood up, flipped the latches on the trunk, lifted the lid and dug her hands underneath the summer clothes at the bottom. The paper envelope with Robin's telephone number was still there. Kookla held it in both hands as she walked toward the phone. She looked at the envelope and then at the phone. She hadn't called Robin for more than a year. Kookla dropped the envelope onto the floor. It landed with the phone number up. She was supposed to call Robin. Kookla started to shiver. The studio felt cold and deserted.

'Deserted except for the boots,' thought Duffer as he entered the floor of his apartment building. There were ten apartments on either side of the corridor. Only three of them had boots outside on the carpet. Duffer kicked the slush off his boots. The walk from Kookla's studio, over icy sidewalks and snowy embankments, had been exhausting. Regardless, he gathered up a neighbour's boots and placed them side by side in the centre of the carpet in the centre of the hallway. He ignored the other boots and unlocked the door to his apartment.

Moving the boots in the hallway had started after the first snowfall, after Duffer had accidentally knocked over a pile of boots belonging to the family next door. There were two large pairs of adult boots and two children's sizes. As a courtesy, Duffer reorganized the family's footwear in descending order from adult to child. The next morning, as he was leaving his apartment, the father smiled at Duffer and thanked him for arranging his doorway. Duffer denied moving the family's boots. He also told the man that his own boots had their tongues pulled out. They had greeted him in the morning, he said, like a couple of panting bulldogs. The neighbor rubbed his chin and re-entered his apartment.

Duffer wasn't really sure why he lied, except that it was partly a joke and partly a way of discouraging conversation. He was worried that the man didn't believe him.

The following morning the residents of the apartment awakened to find that their boots had all been moved. Most of the new arrangements were subtle. One pair of boots had been balanced with its heels on the carpet and its toes on the door. When the door opened, the boots snapped to attention and clicked their heels like an officer in the Luftwaffe. One pair had the inserts reversed, and another had the laces shortened. As the weeks progressed Duffer became more involved with the variations in his work.

Initially, the residents of the floor were amused by the pranks. They would joke about the possible culprit and feign responsibility. In time, however, the joke lost its humour. By the end of the month people were complaining. The superintendent of the building was unable to pursue the matter without a formal report of property damage, so the residents were advised simply to keep their boots inside their apartments.

Once-friendly neighbors were no longer speaking. The air on the floor was mistrustful. Duffer, meanwhile, continued to evade detection. He was patient and methodical and always made certain to include his own boots in the disturbance. At first, the boot moving provided him with a sense of advantage, but this subsided. He began to resent the increasing difficulty of his task. It also felt cowardly.

His end point, he decided, would be the removal of every boot from the hallway. This would represent a final surrender of sorts. Fortunately, only a few stubborn overshoes remained, including his own. A very important consideration occurred to him: the last surviving pair on the floor would become the most suspicious. Duffer needed to withdraw from the contest.

One evening Duffer had opened the door of his apartment and reached for his boots. While doing this he noticed a small Chinese girl sitting in the middle of the hallway. She was wearing a pair of red pyjamas and drinking from a Mason jar. She set the jar between her knees and coughed into her hands. Duffer put down his boots and walked over to the girl. She looked to be about five or six. Beside her, on the carpet, was a colourful pair of boots.

'What are you doing up so late?' he asked.

'I'm waiting for the Boot Mover,' she said.

Duffer felt ashamed. 'It sounds like you have a bad cough. You should go back to bed.'

The girl shook her head and presented the Mason jar. 'This is my medicine for asthma.' The container was half filled with a brown liquid. A thick sediment had settled on the bottom.

'What's in the water?'

The girl rotated the jar and the sediment lifted. To his surprise, a team of tiny seahorses reared up. They galloped around in the tea as if linked to a carousel. Duffer asked for the Mason jar.

'You have to show me something first,' she said.

'Will you go to sleep afterwards?'

'Yes.'

Duffer was wearing only a pair of wool socks, a white cotton T-shirt and his pyjama bottoms. He had nothing to show her. At first he tried improvising some shadow puppets on a wall using his fingers and a coverless fire-door bulb. The little girl had no reaction. He then shaped his hands into an ocarina and performed a little puffing song on the knuckles of his thumbs. The little girl yawned. Duffer made a final survey of the hallway. He attempted one last trick.

'Stick out your finger,' he told her.

'Like this?'

'That's right.'

Duffer marched to the end of the corridor. He then turned around and shuffled back toward the girl, dragging his wool-stockinged feet on the carpet.

'Are you ready?' he asked her.

'Ready for what?'

Duffer touched the girl's extended finger and discharged a snapping blue volt of electricity. She yelped and fell backwards. Suddenly, there was the sound of anxious footsteps from behind an apartment door. Duffer dashed back into his apartment, locked the door and waited for the angry knock and the trouble that would follow. He waited and worried, but nothing happened.

He was unable to sleep. In the morning, Duffer was certain, he would be evicted. He might also be cited for mischief and trespassing. In any event, the residents of the apartment would be informed of his activities and he would be held accountable. He was nervous when entering and exiting the apartment. And he stopped moving the boots.

A week straggled past without a word from the landlord. Eventually, Duffer's uneasiness began to subside. He was hopeful that the little girl had never mentioned his visit. Even if she had, he reminded himself, she had never actually seen him move any of the boots. A second uneventful week helped to bolster his confidence. Finally, by the end of the third week, Duffer felt reassured. He turned his attention back to the boots.

During his absence the boots had crept back into the corridor like a herd of thirsty animals to an unprotected watering hole. Duffer was still afraid of getting caught, but the return of the footwear represented a disregard for his domain. He decided to thin out the herd.

He started with the little girl's boots. He held the right boot in his hand; it was the size of a drinking glass. Inside he found a rolled-up piece of paper. He took the paper, dropped the boot and rushed back into his apartment.

Duffer locked his door. He was so tired from walking back from Kookla's, and from arguing with her, that he decided to go straight to bed. It was almost six in the morning. He took off his overcoat and let it slump over the side of the couch. He tossed his keys, change and gum onto a table like he was feeding the pigeons. Then he stopped for a moment. He walked into his kitchen and turned on the light. He stood there looking at the refrigerator. The little girl's present, a picture of the Boot Mover, was attached to the fridge door. The drawing was in crayon. It showed a smiling underwater creature floating through the hallway with a multitude of legs. Its stringy feet were covered with a dozen pairs of woolly socks. Surrounding the creature's body was an energetic display of silver zigzags that suggested either lightning bolts or electricity. It was the gentle creature's natural means of protection.

Protective adhesive from the nicotine patch was stuck to Igor's skin. Autumn peeled it away and looked even closer at the mark on Igor's shoulder. It was a tattoo. The tattoo was outlined in black smudging pigment. Its contours were fleshy and raised above the skin's surface, not unlike the texture of a scrambled egg.

From a distance it might have passed for a birthmark. Igor clicked the lighter shut.

'That's a nasty-looking tattoo,' said Autumn.

'It is not so bothering me.'

'Why is it so rough?'

Igor dropped the lighter back onto the pile of clothes on the floor. 'Because I was unconscious at time.'

'You were unconscious?' asked Autumn.

'It was a quick job,' he said. 'Artist must have been worried that I am to awaken during application. One can tell by clumsiness of work.' Igor placed a hand over the top of the swollen markings. 'The heaviness of the wound it comes from keloids.'

'Meaning?'

'It is meaning that scar is still spreading and corrupting image.'

Autumn combed his fingers through his hair. His scalp was itchy from lying on Igor's mattress. 'How did this happen?'

'Robin helped his friend organize after-hours club for drinking.'

'A booze can?'

'Yes. A good friend of Robin's was in need of cash. Robin helped his friend with organizing booze can. They are partners, Robin making the location and the friend inviting guests.'

'Who was this friend?'

'I don't know. I never met him. I think he is friend of Robin from medical school. I'm not so sure how Kookla knows him.'

'Did Kookla help?'

'No. She wanted nothing to do with Medicine Show.'

'Medicine Show, that's a funny name for the event.'

'You understand,' explained Igor, 'it is illegal for drinking after hours, location for booze can is big secret.'

'Of course.'

'Robin had good idea, make it in centre of city, location with it expected for people to come at night.'

'Where was it?'

'In hospital anatomy lab.'

'You must be joking!'

Igor smiled and shook his head. 'Robin is hospital personnel with access, he opens back door for friend, a bouncer he stays at door for guests … the Medicine Show.'

'What did Kookla have to say about this?'

'She was angry with Robin.'

'Did she ask you to go?'

'Yes, I am promising to look after Robin.' Igor lay on the bed with his hands behind his head. 'That night I am arriving in alley behind teaching hospital with others. These people are drunk and shouting and knocking at entrance. We wait until doorman opens door. He is muscular fellow with telephone and dark glasses. After he is taking our money and patting our coats, we are taken inside.'

'What was it like inside?'

'It is dark and we are crowded together. We are guided by flashlight through many small rooms with rattling shelves. Then, as we get closer to party, the air is start smelling of formalin and cigarettes. The sounds of conversation and music are getting louder. We are now in anatomy lab, big open room, low ceilings. The floor is made from ceramic tile. It is hard to see inside except for wet samples in jars that are making some lighting.'

'Wet samples – do you mean dissections?'

'Yes, dissections, they are with illumination. Much of the crowd is near bar. The bar is metal stretcher underneath lamps for making surgery. People are talking and resting their drinks on stainless-steel cabinets for holding the cadaver. Skeletons on poles, like nervous girls at first dance, are together in one corner. There is also large chalkboard on wheels at bar with prices for drinks and diagram of liver.'

'It sounds weird,' said Autumn.

'There are musicians with powdered faces. They are playing on accordion, violin and flute. A shrouded figure is dancing with music wearing wetted cheesecloth, like anatomists use to keep cadavers moist. All I could see underneath material was small gap at abdomen.'

'Could you tell if the person was a man or a woman?'

'I could not tell. The stomach was smooth like woman's, but, to be honest, I am already much drunk at this time.'

'Where was Robin?'

'Robin is sitting quietly on large branching reproduction of vertebra. I stumble toward him and fall on my ass. Robin he laughs. He is lifting me off floor by my wrists. I am drawn into his arms and we are making a long embrace. *Mēs sveicinājam kā matroži.* We are greeting like sailors. I remember that he smelled of alcohol.'

'And then what happened?'

'Robin he introduced me to a friend.'

'The partner you mentioned earlier?'

'No, not the partner – it is a man's nervous system suspended in saline. He is saying to me that this is his undergraduate project. We are looking at shallow tank, and floating in water is brain with spinal cord and nerves. The nerves, they are extending into shrivelled hands and feet, like creature is wearing stockings and gloves made from flesh. It is horrible, I tell him. I cannot remember if I am throwing up.'

'Why did Robin want to show you this thing?'

'I'm not sure. He said something like creature is floating free of pain and sensation in sterile brine. He talked about it for long time. But I am not listening.' Igor stopped and looked at Autumn. 'I am ashamed to say what is happened next.'

'Go ahead,' said Autumn.

Igor hesitated. 'I wake up on medical table. Dividers with white curtains are in circle around my body. My head is so hurting, I am sick in the stomach, and the shirt from my left shoulder is sticking to table with blood. I am falling off table and on floor. When I open up curtains I am alone in anatomy lab. All that is left is cups and bottles and cigarette butts. It is important for me to leave as quickly as possible. As I am rushing for back door is when I am stepping on human hand … '

'Was it from a specimen jar?'

'No, it was Robin's hand, he was lying on floor naked and unconscious.'

'What did you do?'

Igor turned his face away from Autumn. 'I am leaving him on the floor.'

Autumn was speechless.

'What else could I have done?' he asked. 'It is morning, he is unconscious, and I am to walk from hospital anatomy lab carrying naked body?'

'You just left him there,' he said, 'despite your promise to Kookla?'

Igor pressed his fists against his temples. 'Robin was admitted to own hospital with diagnosis of alcohol toxicity. He was suspended from program. A probation for him was discussed with administrators, but he declined. After this he was never to practice again medicine. This is maybe year and a half ago. It is just before you are together with Kookla. After this, you understand, she is working in garage for only short time and then quitting.'

Autumn climbed out of the bed and collected his clothing. He quietly dressed and prepared for a walk to the studio. He suddenly knew it was urgent that he talk with Kookla. 'Does she know about your tattoo,' he asked, 'or how you found Robin?'

'No, she made visit to him in hospital, and he told her nothing about the evening, nothing except that I am good friend. Kookla did not believe him and is thinking that I am too drunk and careless. This is much better for her to know than real explanation. That purpose of evening is to make Robin dismissed from medical program.'

'Someone must have tampered with your drinks.'

'I think you are right,' considered Igor. 'It is to make harm on Robin. I am certain of this. My tattoo it is maybe a warning. A warning to not interfere.'

'How can you be certain when the tattoo has lost its image?'

'You are forgetting about my shirt,' said Igor. 'The blood stain on fabric it is a composite of tattoo. I know what image is.'

'Well,' he asked, 'what is it?'

'It is a snake and underneath snake a Japanese character.'

'Are you sure?' Autumn asked. 'The bottom part looks more like a scribble or a stab mark.'

'I am certain,' said Igor. 'One of my mechanics is from Kamuno, Japan. The character, he is explaining, means white.'

'White?'

'Yes, and the character for white,' continued Igor, 'it is also meaning innocent.'

'Innocent mistake,' drawled the voice on the phone. 'Just don't call me so early in the morning next time.'

'Sorry, Monkeyblood,' apologized Kookla, 'I thought this was Robin's telephone number.'

'It was,' Monkeyblood yawned. He cracked his neck.

'Do you know where he is?'

'How come you don't know his number?'

'We broke up more than a year ago.'

'I see, well, I don't have his number, but I know that he moved into the apartment building across the street from the chocolate factory.'

'I know the building.'

'He moved out of here almost six months ago. It was nice of him to let me have his place. He even let me keep his piano.'

'How are things going?' she asked. 'We haven't spoken for a long time.'

'I'm good,' he said. 'I'm working right now with a photo-bioscope.' His voice lifted somewhat. 'It's about a hundred and fifty years old and it's imported from England. If you're interested I can get you a ticket to the performance.'

'What's a photobioscope?' Kookla asked.

'It's a projector, or a reflector, I'm not sure how else to describe it. The contraption sits in the middle of the theatre with an extension on the roof and reflects an image of the outside world on the inside walls.'

'Like a spy glass?'

'Sort of ... but the image gets distorted. For example, an everyday scene, like an automobile passing over a bridge or a person shovelling the sidewalk, it looks different. It almost looks like an early movie. My job is to improvise a composition that accompanies the image.'

'It sounds wonderful,' she said. 'It must feel like you're watching a memory or a dream.'

'Yeah, it kind of feels like that.'

'I'm sure that Robin would enjoy the show.'

'I doubt it. Robin never held a high opinion of my work as an accompanist.'

'He loved your silent movie shows,' remembered Kookla.

'He loved the Vitagraph cue sheets,' he said. 'After the movies he'd sit on the bench with me and we'd perform songs like "Pot Boiling" and "Baby Crying" and "Horse Galloping." His favourite film scores incorporated classical themes – the same kind of themes he used in his later compositions.'

'What compositions?'

'The stuff that he left behind. It was very technical – it sounded to me like he was trying to work through a math problem.'

'Did he perform these for you?'

'No, I found them, the sheet music. They were inside the piano bench underneath a collection of tapes he labelled "The Library of Forgotten Sounds."'

'What's on them?'

'Forgotten sounds: a rotary telephone, a typewriter, the bell of a streetcar. I have no idea what it means. Although, to be honest, I do find the recordings very beautiful and nostalgic.'

'Did you come across anything else?' asked Kookla.

'Like what?'

'Well, he used to keep a journal, but I can't find it anywhere.'

Monkeyblood tried to remember. He pressed down on his orbits with the flats of his fingers. A geometric pattern blossomed against the backs of his retinas. 'Not that I can recall,' he said. The black and white kaleidoscopes faded.

'Too bad,' she said.

'What are you looking for?' he asked. Monkeyblood adjusted the telephone receiver between his ear and shoulder.

The extension held a silence for a moment. 'For some kind of explanation … '

'Don't bother,' he finally said. 'I've known Robin for years, since we were kids, and I still can't understand why his affection toward me is so … determined.'

'Why do you say that? Did he do something to hurt you?'

'I'm not sure. It happened a long time ago. When we were students at the Academy of Arts and Sciences. I think we were sixteen at the time.'

'What happened?'

'Robin was the better student – he always did well on his music exams and excelled in other subjects like biology, math and chemistry. By the end of the year he had graduated with honours and I had failed. In fact, I couldn't pass the school year without an extra summer course in music theory. This meant that we couldn't spend our summer together.'

'He told me that you went camping.'

'That's true, but we planned something different that year, a trip to the Old Banner Theater in Los Angeles to see the orchestrion.

'What's an orchestrion?'

'It's a giant music box. The one in Los Angeles is over ten feet tall and six feet wide. It was built in 1910 and its sculpted wooden cabinet contained a piano, three sections of organ pipes, base and snare drums, cymbals, triangles, tambourines and a thirty-bar xylophone.'

'What was it supposed to do?'

'It was supposed to accompany silent movies.'

'Why haven't I heard of these things before?'

'When the talking pictures arrived, the orchestrion became obsolete. They were too big and too complex to dismantle so the theatre owners just tore them apart. One exception is the Old Banner, where it was hidden behind a brick wall and accidentally uncovered during restorations.'

'Did it work?' she asked.

'It worked just fine – they plugged it in and it played "A Bicycle Built for Two." I can only imagine how those workmen must have felt when that machine was started up and the theatre filled with music from a hundred years ago.' Monkeyblood paused and returned to his story. 'Anyhow, we were disappointed, and Robin was angry with me. But he was even angrier with the Academy. It had a standard of excellence to maintain, I understood this, but it troubled Robin, and he was anxious to prove his friendship.'

'What did he do?'

'He sabotaged the Academy's grand piano.'

'How?'

'He figured out a way to keep the piano out of tune. It was ingenious, because it happened only after he left the Academy. You see, the piano has hundreds of strings, and each string is attached to a metal pin that requires constant tuning. When the pin is properly tuned, a liquid called pin tightener is applied that prevents it from drifting. Robin simply switched this liquid for his own solution, a mixture of antifreeze and salt, which formed an extremely corrosive and oxidizing combination. When his solution was applied to the pins they quickly rusted and pulled the strings out of tune.'

'Couldn't they just tune the piano again?'

'They tried, but the rusted pins cracked with each tuning. It was terrible. He killed that piano one string at a time. I felt different about Robin after that. We stopped spending our summers together.'

'I'm sorry if I woke you up,' Kookla said, suddenly wanting to get off the phone. 'Maybe I'll drop by that building you mentioned and see if he's around.'

'If he isn't there,' said Monkeyblood, 'let me know. There's one other place he might be.'

'Where's that?'

'The directions are too complicated to give over the phone.' Monkeyblood turned his face away from the receiver and looked at his alarm clock. 'Damn it,' he cursed, 'I gotta get up in a couple of hours.'

'Would you care to join me?' she asked. 'Maybe we can visit Robin together.'

Monkeyblood thought about it for a while. 'No thanks,' he said finally. 'I'll pass.'

A passing city snowplough with flashing blue lights scraped and rumbled over the roadside. Robin left the sidewalk, climbed over a boot-sucking snowdrift and walked onto a cleared strip of asphalt. It was six in the morning. The buses were running and the city was beginning to stir. Robin was only a few minutes away from Kookla's studio.

Years ago, when he was still in the medical program, he would finish his shift, complete his rounds and rush home before

Kookla awakened. He remembered one time, almost two years ago, when he got home around this time. He undressed in the bedroom and crawled under the covers with her.

'Hands off,' shivered Kookla, 'you're freezing!'

'I'm sorry,' he apologized. 'I didn't mean to wake you.' He kissed the nape of her neck. 'Go back to sleep.' His arms slipped around her waist.

'Why are you home so late?'

'Surgery,' he said. 'I've just graduated to first assistant.'

'That's good. When's your next shift?'

'Noon today,' he mumbled. His face was in the pillow.

Kookla tightened her body against Robin. She could feel the coolness of his hands resting on her bare stomach. She listened to the sound of his breathing.

'I had an unusual experience this evening,' he finally said.

'What happened?'

'My patient with the intractable seizures – we call him Mr J – we were mapping out his brain with a cranial stimulator when suddenly, in the middle of the operation, he told us to stop.'

'He's awake?'

'Yes, he needs to be awake; otherwise we can't identify his language sites.'

'Why did he tell you to stop?'

'Because Mr J felt a presence.'

Kookla opened her eyes. 'What kind of presence?'

'He said an incredible presence had entered the room.'

'What did he mean?'

'I have no idea what he meant. I don't think anybody in the operating room knew what he meant. We all glanced at each other from behind our masks and tried to figure out what was going on. After a few minutes of stalling, the Chief Surgeon asked Mr J if he could actually see the presence. Mr J explained that the presence was in the operating room but it was not something that he could see. The surgeon explained that his perception of a presence was the result of electrical stimulation to his cortex, or maybe even a mild seizure, and that it was still in his best interest to continue with the operation. Mr J told the surgeon to stop.'

'What happened next?'

'The surgeon had to contact the hospital's Ethics Commissioner. The Ethics Commissioner listened to the case and contacted the hospital lawyer. The surgeon, the lawyer and the Ethics Commissioner discussed Mr J and his ability to make an informed decision. The three of them spoke for about thirty minutes using the operating room intercom. They even spoke with Mr J who responded to their questions with his head screwed into the metal ring of a Sagitta holder. During the conversation I irrigated the exposed portion of his brain with normal saline. The tumour was sitting right there – we could have removed it, but in the end we reapplied the dura, sutured on the circular bone flap, replaced the bone dust in the bur holes and stapled down the scalp. Mr J was then transferred to the recovery room with his tumour in situ.'

'Maybe it isn't such a bad thing,' said Kookla. 'Who knows – maybe your patient's perception of an incredible presence was real?'

'It wasn't real,' argued Robin. 'It was the result of a surgeon directing an electrical current to a particular part of his brain. We were working on his left temporal lobe. It's an area that's associated with religious thinking. Patients with epileptic seizures originating from this part of the brain often have intense spiritual experiences and sometimes become preoccupied with religious thoughts even after the seizures have passed.'

'Did Mr J ever experience this incredible presence during one of his seizures?'

Robin thought for a moment. 'No,' he replied. 'At least it was never reported.'

'Maybe Mr J became aware of something undetected as a

result of this stimulation to his brain. The electric needle may have simply heightened the sensitivity of his brain cells that are responsible for the perception of the divine. It's like when you burn your tongue on something hot and afterwards the taste of everything is intensified.'

'I understand your argument,' said Robin. 'But it isn't something that you can prove or disprove scientifically.'

'There are things that go on that are beyond our senses.' Kookla's voice was beginning to strain. 'I know this because, even within myself, there are things … '

Robin could hear that Kookla was crying. He brushed the hair from her face and touched her cheek. 'Listen,' he said quietly, 'we can talk about this later.'

'No,' she said, turning toward him. 'I'm tired of being sick.'
'I know.'
'Whatever is troubling me is lost to my senses.'
'I know,' he repeated.

Kookla rested her head on Robin's chest and rubbed the tears from her eyes. 'I'm sorry,' she said. 'I wasn't expecting that.'

'Don't worry.' He touched Kookla's hand and felt the teardrops on her fingers.

'What's going to happen to Mr J?' she asked.

'If he's found to be competent, Mr J can refuse his surgery. If the Ethics Committee determines that Mr J is incompetent, then he might have to undergo a procedure that could neutralize the part of his brain that's affecting his ability to make an informed decision.'

'How's that possible?' asked Kookla. 'You just told me that you're not allowed to perform any surgery on Mr J unless he gives you permission.'

'It isn't a surgical procedure,' said Robin. 'We use a device called the transcranial magnetic stimulator. When it's applied to the patient's head it emits a rapidly fluctuating and extremely powerful magnetic field that can be directed at any particular part of the brain. It all depends on what part of the brain you want to stimulate.'

'Wouldn't that device simply increase the patient's symptoms?'

'Yes, but it would also allow for a process called "flooding," where the sensitized tissue becomes overloaded. When the tissue is overloaded, its effects on the brain are temporarily removed. Following this procedure Mr J would undergo further psychiatric testing. If he's found to be competent then he can decide on his surgery.'

'It sounds like your device is expected to change his decision.'

'It has nothing to do with decision-making,' said Robin. 'It has more to do with disconnecting the damaged cells from his brain temporarily. The machine was originally developed as an instrument for brain mapping. For example, if I were to stimulate you here,' Robin tapped his index finger against Kookla's right temple, 'your right eye would wink at me.'

'What if you stimulated me here?' Kookla pointed a finger to the top of her head in the manner of a pirouette.

Robin laughed. 'If the beam struck your thalamus you'd have an orgasm.'

Kookla smiled. She then lifted her head up from Robin's chest. He could tell that she was thinking about something important.

'What is it?' he asked.

'Robin,' she said, 'if you were to try and disconnect me from my memories … '

'I doesn't work like that,' he said. 'And even if it did, the effects of the stimulator are only temporary.'

'I know, but if you tried … where would you touch me?'

Robin hesitated. He then placed his finger against Kookla's left eyebrow. 'Here.'

Kookla took hold of Robin's hand. She slowly drew it toward her lips and kissed his extended finger.

'I love you,' she said.

'I love you, too.'

Kookla rested her head on Robin's chest, her ear against his heart as if she were listening for the sea in a conch shell. His pulse, like a tide, carried her off into sleep. In the morning Robin was gone.

A bundle of newspapers struck the pavement beside Robin's feet and startled him out of his memory. He quickly stepped aside from the curb and watched as the newspaper van rushed up the street and rolled out another bundle. People were beginning to appear on the street. A man was salting the sidewalk in front of a bakery. A woman with a briefcase was brushing the snow from her car windshield. A busload of sleeping shift workers was arriving at a bus stop. A young woman boarding the bus caught his attention and he realized that it was Kookla. He shouted her name and started running after the bus. After sliding on the icy road and falling to the ground, he gave up the chase. He got up, dusted the snow from his pants and followed the bus with his eyes as it passed through an intersection and disappeared.

Robin decided to continue on toward the studio. He wasn't entirely certain that the woman on the bus was Kookla. When he arrived, he walked up the snow-covered steps and tried her buzzer. He waited but there was no reply. Robin sat down and thought about where she might have gone. His footsteps, he realized, had smudged Duffer's name spelled out in piss in the snow.

'Snowplough on your left,' alerted Autumn.

'I know, I know,' replied Igor. 'Allow me for one moment.' Igor skidded the Mistress in front of the snowplough, stopped the car, and rolled down his window. He shouted in Latvian at the driver of the snowplough. The driver rolled down his window and started shouting back. A few minutes of arguing ensued, and then they started laughing. Igor cranked up his car window and reversed the automobile. The driver of the snowplough directed a friendly wave at Igor and returned to his work.

'Do you Latvians enjoy arguing?' asked Autumn.

Igor was still laughing to himself. 'I am knowing this asshole from research institute in Riga. He is expert in fuel development, very important, making fuel from water.'

'Is that possible?'

'Is very possible.' Igor tapped his cigarette ash. 'Water is hydrogen and oxygen, yes? Both elements are … to make a flame?'

'Combustible?'

'Combustible. This man and research team separating elements from water with accelerator process – I do not understand process but they are successful. Suddenly there is no more fuel program and he is to leaving Latvia.' Igor smiled and remembered his little joke. 'I am asking him now if he is testing new fuel cells in snowplough.'

'Why is he an asshole?'

'He is asshole,' he said around the cigarette in his mouth, 'because he is telling me that he is going home after work and is to fuck my wife.'

'He's joking,' said Autumn.

'He is not joking.'

'What are you talking about?'

'I am married,' said Igor. 'Of course my wife is now living with this man. That is why I am coming to this country, for chasing after wife, but she will not have me. I am leaving behind everything in Riga. Still, it is not enough, or maybe is too much.' He stroked the car's dashboard affectionately. 'Now I am only with second woman. That is why I am calling her the Mistress.'

'How long were you married?'

'Maybe ten years. My wife, her name is Annila, she is also from Latvia and she is also engineer.'

'Why did you separate?'

'It is the same for every couple – I was not happy and she was not happy.'

'Is it really that simple?'

'Yes,' answered Igor. 'It is that simple.'

'I don't know,' wavered Autumn.

'Why did you leave Kookla?' asked Igor.

'What makes you think it was me who left Kookla?'

A row of stationed taxicabs attracted Igor's attention. He let up on the accelerator and allowed the Mistress to coast in beside the parking lot. 'Do you think the taxicabs are propane?' He stopped the car and searched the parking lot for signs of patrolling guard dogs.

'Answer me,' Autumn said. 'Why would you think it was me who left Kookla?'

'Maybe Kookla could not do what you ask and this is what makes you unhappy and you decide to leave.'

'What did I ask?'

'Maybe you ask Kookla to act like she is healthy.'

'What are you saying?' Autumn's voice was angry.

'Do not feel so bad about this,' consoled Igor. 'I am also trying to help Kookla, and also Robin before you, but for Kookla to hear that something is always wrong … '

'I only remember telling Kookla once that I was worried about her … ' Autumn struggled for the word, 'her behaviour.'

Igor laughed and shook his head. 'It is more than one time,' he said. 'Do you not know the story of Hans the Counting Horse?'

'Oh, for Chrissake, Igor.'

'No, no,' he said. 'Listen – this will make sense to you. In early twentieth century was German horse named Hans that counts numbers.'

'Is this a fable?'

'No, is true story, now please to stop interrupting. Wilhelm Von Osten, who is retired mathematician, he presents counting horse to scientific community. Horse and Von Osten appear onstage together. Von Osten, who is wearing lab coat, is drawing big white numbers on chalkboard. Hans is counting numbers on chalkboard and striking ground with hoof with correct answer. Is no difference if Von Osten asks question or if audience member asks question. The counting horse is always answering correctly.'

'I don't believe it.'

'Von Osten claimed counting horse is genuine scientific discovery. European scientists make "Hans Commission," investigate horse's abilities, and after months of testing conclude that Hans is able to problem solving mathematics. Hans is called marvel of century until scientist named Pfungst he is announcing that he can disclaim counting horse. In his experiment an idiot, who could not understand numbers, is presenting math problem. They discover if examiner is not understanding numbers, counting horse cannot count.'

'Why are you telling me this?'

'Don't you see? The counting horse could not count. He could perform task guided by investigator's facial expression or body language or unspoken cues. Whatever is explanation, this horse, who is not of our species, who has no understanding of mathematics, he is able to satisfy examiner. Why? Because examiner believes he can accomplish task.'

'I was only trying to help Kookla.'

'But you did not help Kookla,' he said. 'You left her.'

'I had to leave her.'

'I am not interested,' said Igor. 'I am knowing Kookla is troubled, but is from Robin, he is also trying to help her when they are together.'

'How?'

'How … more than two years ago, when I am walking into office at garage, I see Robin sitting on floor in front of cigarette machine. There is tape recorder on floor beside him. He is hold-ing microphone against the machine. I am about to say, "Robin, what are you doing?" when he gestures for me to be quiet. He holds up one finger in front of his lips and narrows eyes. He then pulls knob on machine and cigarettes tumble down. Robin turns off tape recorder, gets up from floor and tosses me package of cigarettes.'

'What was he doing?'

'He is recording cigarette machine for Library of Forgotten Sounds. Robin is telling me that tape recorder, with its buttons and tape hiss, is also becoming forgotten sound.'

'Why was he collecting these sounds?'

'He was collecting them for Kookla.'

'Why?'

'To help her to learn to control memories better. She is very troubled from separation with past. It is not by her choice, it is a sickness of memory, but it is also a protection. That is why Robin is to collect forgotten sounds. He is thinking it is functioning like a stimulus. I could see that Robin is desperate. He is afraid Kookla might hurt herself. He is also afraid that he might hurt Kookla with trying to help her. That is why he is to leave her.'

Igor decided to ignore the row of parked taxicabs. He thrust the gears into drive and merged the Mistress back into traffic.

'Did Kookla ever talk to you about our relationship?'

'How do you mean?'

'When we were together,' Autumn said, 'when we were intimate, there was an absence. It felt like she wasn't there. I even-tually mentioned this feeling of absence to her.'

'What did she say?'

'She couldn't explain it. She tried. But all she could say was that having sex was like breathing underwater.'

'What did she mean?'

Autumn shook his head. 'Yesterday evening, after we had made love, I awakened to find myself alone in bed. It was late at night and the studio was dark. I called out for Kookla but she didn't answer, so I got out of bed and walked toward the washroom. The door was closed but the light was on. I knocked and said, "Kookla, are you in there?" but again there was no answer. When I opened the door I found her sitting naked on the edge of the bathtub. I asked her what she was doing but she didn't respond. I realized that Kookla's left hand was covered in blood. She sat there, ignoring me, snipping at the skin in between her fingers with a metal nail clipper. I ran over and grabbed it from her hand. At first, she didn't seem to recognize me, so I shouted and shook her by the shoulders. Suddenly her expression changed. She looked at me and smiled as if to say "What are you doing here?" She then looked down at her hand, staring in disbelief at the blood between her fingers. She began to cry, her hands over her eyes, and she withdrew to the farthest corner of the bathtub. I approached her calmly, separated her fingers and her toes, examined the flesh underneath her arms, and checked behind her ears and inside her mouth. I found that Kookla was covered with hidden scars.'

'Why would she do this to herself?'

'She said that it helps her to feel something. It comforts her to see the cuts and feel the pain. She also told me that it brings her back.'

'Back from what?'

'I don't know.'

Igor quietly finished his cigarette and tossed the butt into traffic. He searched through his jacket pockets for another package of smokes. 'I will have to stop and get more cigarettes.'

'We're almost at the studio,' Autumn said. 'It'll be faster if you drop me off around the back.'

Igor bounded the car over a snow-covered speed bump and into the studio's back lot, which was empty except for a large metal waste bin and two massive wooden spools. Topped with snow, the spools looked like two lonely tables set with linen. Igor parked the car and shut off the engine. He took off his seat belt, turned his body sideways and looked at Autumn.

'Did you leave Kookla after learning she is hurting herself?'

'Yes, so she wouldn't have to contend with the demands of a relationship.'

'You cannot be helping someone if you are not around.'

'I understand that,' he said. 'And that's why I've come back.'

'So what are you going to do now?'

'I don't know.'

They sat quietly in the car and listened to the muffled pings of the cooling engine. 'Do you really want to help Kookla?' asked Igor.

'Yes.'

'Then you must try and protect her,' he said. 'And for you to protect her you must do something terrible. I do not have the courage to do this for her.'

'And what's that?'

'The first thing you must do is find Robin.'

'And then?'

'And then after you find Robin you must kill him.'

'I'd kill for a half-decent coffee right now,' thought Duffer as he stared at his tired-looking face in the medicine-cabinet mirror. The mirror was connected to the cabinet with four crescent-shaped brackets that looked like grey fingernails. The long, confusing night at Kookla's had taken its toll. Duffer opened the door and removed a small rectangular compact from the shelf. He closed the door with a click and touched a finger to his lip.

The top right vermilion of his lip was swollen where Kookla had scratched him. Duffer cursed and opened the compact. A touch of the applicator brush cooled his lip. While he was smoothing it down his eyes focused on a reflection of a wall calendar. A number on the calendar was underlined with red. It was the date of his audition.

'Oh shit!' His hands tightened against the sides of the porcelain sink. 'I was supposed to have an original piece ready for today.' The audition required a five-minute monologue recounting a personal experience.

'What am I going to do?' Duffer glared uncertainly at the reflection of the calendar. The numbers and letters were reversed. It was six in the morning and he had only a couple of hours to prepare before the audition. The makeup was making his lip sting, which reminded him of Kookla. The reversed date in the mirror reminded him of the time when he was teaching her photography. It was the time he had felt closest to her.

Kookla and Autumn had been taking a drawing class together while they were dating. Autumn was the more experienced of the two, as he had nearly completed a four-year program in Fine Arts. Kookla enjoyed the classes but had difficulties with composition. For some reason, if she rendered more than one object on the page, the elements never seemed to have any relationship with one another. The instructor told her that it was a problem with framing.

Autumn tried to show her different methods of framing a composition. Despite his best efforts, Kookla's resistance worsened and the drawings became even more strange and isolating. Finally, Duffer suggested that Kookla study composition through another medium. He recommended photography because the camera would help to consolidate an image within a given frame.

Duffer provided Kookla with a camera. She learned how to use it and quickly developed a new appreciation for light and movement, especially the signature of a moving light source through darkness. It all began with one lucky photograph that Duffer snapped of Kookla in the rain. She had been completely drenched, her hair painted flat to her head and her clothes sticking to her skin. It was an unremarkable photograph except for the small white eruption beside her.

'What is this thing?' she asked.

Duffer smiled. 'It was pretty dark under the clouds,' he said. 'So I had to increase the exposure time of the film. That's why I told you to stand perfectly still. All of a sudden this little white dog dripped his way into the picture.'

'This doesn't look like a dog.'

'It's a dog,' said Duffer. 'He's shaking off the raindrops.'

Kookla was fascinated by the strangeness of the photograph, its contrasting stillness and motion. She decided to investigate more possibilities. Duffer managed to procure a tripod.

The majority of Kookla's photographs were disappointing, but she and Duffer persisted. They would hang around together in the evenings and wait for something, whatever that might be, to happen.

After several weeks of determined shooting, a couple of good photographs emerged. The first one was taken at the trolley car junction, where a half-circle turn at the end of the route conducted the vehicles onto a parallel track. At night the streetcars would coast along the metal rails of the cement platform with their lights off. A few metres above the cement floor of the platform dangled a cat's cradle of electrical wires, which flickered with every pluck of the streetcar's aerial. The most resounding contact occurred at the exit, where a dip in the track disengaged the aerial from the wire. With every jolt on the wire a tremendous *pop* sounded and sparks showered out. It was a reliable shot. So Kookla and Duffer set up the camera and waited. The camera, with its bulging glass eye, recorded every flash of light from every passing streetcar. And the photo turned out even better than they expected. In the centre of the station, suspended above the cement floor of the platform, was a dripping fireworks display that resembled a melting chandelier.

The second good photograph occurred by accident. Kookla and Duffer were walking along the waterfront. They stopped on the embankment and sat down, kicking their legs back and forth over the water and talking. They were interrupted by the cry of a siren. An ambulance appeared, careened around a corner and then vanished. Duffer leaned over the railing and looked after the ambulance. A few blocks away, at the foot of the pier, a group of emergency vehicles had gathered. Kookla and Duffer collected their equipment.

The area was crowded with police officers and firefighters. The uniformed men were speaking into walkie-talkies and positioning road flares. Neither Duffer nor Kookla could identify the source of the excitement. They did notice, however, that everyone's attention seemed to be focused on a small section of broken fence.

Kookla and Duffer walked over to the fence and leaned over the railing. Two elliptical shapes were burning bright underneath the water. Beside one of the shapes was an orange light, which was blinking on and off. It was a car, and its signal light was still blinking underwater.

Duffer uncapped the camera and passed it over to Kookla. They got in about three minutes of exposure time before a policeman chased them away.

A luminous spot in the centre of the photograph outlined the windshield of the sunken car. Through the windshield, if the photograph was held at a certain angle, one could see a pair of grey hands resting on a steering wheel.

The most unusual of Kookla's photos were taken outside the women's prison. Kookla was attracted to the area not because of the detention centre but because of a nearby construction site with its rotating cranes and their Christmas-light decorations. While Kookla busied herself with the camera, Duffer inspected the prison. The architecture was severe in its simplicity – a square rampart with square windows arrayed in a square pattern. At the top of the grid, adjacent to a sharpened corner, was a light. Duffer poked repeatedly at Kookla's shoulder until she turned around and looked at the building. They watched the light inside the window twirl around like a firebug in a jar.

The sequence of the light was the same: a five-second light, a brief interruption, a five-second light, a brief interruption, and so on. Neither Duffer nor Kookla could make any sense of the tracings.

'Is it a signal of some kind?' asked Duffer.

'Who knows?'

They waited for another hour but the light did not return.

'Let's try again tomorrow night,' she said.

They returned the following night and the night after that, but there was no recurrence of the light. Nevertheless, they continued to set up the camera. It was another week to the day before the sketchy prison light finally reappeared. Kookla held down on the shutter release with every five seconds of light and advanced the film forward with every interruption. When the lights finally stopped, the counter read twenty photographs.

'There were twenty different patterns,' Kookla said. 'Any ideas what it means?'

'No idea,' Duffer said. 'But the individual strokes all look different to me, like a semaphore. I think we need to keep them in that order. We'll have to make a contact sheet.'

The contact sheet displayed the twenty photographs in their consecutive order.

9J3A23 70AƆ)V3M393T3A

The unexpected message left them baffled.

'Why would she write out the letters in reverse?' asked Duffer. 'It only makes the message more difficult to read.'

'I don't think it was meant for us to read,' Kookla said. 'And I doubt it's for Peter to read, if he's alive. She probably writes it out for herself, once a week, as an act of atonement. It's our perspective from outside her window that reverses the letters.'

'But why once a week?' asked Duffer. 'Why not every night, or every other night for that matter?'

Kookla rubbed a finger underneath her bottom lip. She looked around the studio. Her eyes eventually settled on a kitchen drawer. From its clutter she removed a book of matches. She struck a match and wrote the letter 'P' on the air. The duration of the match's burn was about five seconds. It was much too long for Kookla to hold. She dropped the smoking match and sucked her burned fingers. Duffer recovered the matchbook.

'There are twenty matches,' he counted.

'And twenty letters in the sentence. The woman in the prison window has to wait a week between messages for her fingers to heal.'

Duffer remembered passing Kookla a cold cloth for her fingers.

Now he dampened a cold cloth for himself, letting it soak up the water from the sink and holding it against his face. He was careful not to smudge the makeup on his lip. Despite his initial panic, the reflected number on the bathroom calendar had turned out to be a lucky number. The matchbook experience would work out well for the audition. He decided to rehearse his new piece in front of the mirror. The monologue, he thought, would be even more convincing if he were the person reaching out from the prison cell.

Cellophane wrap choked the hallway smoke detectors. Autumn thought it was odd. He looked down from the ceiling to the floor and found an empty cardboard cylinder at his feet.

He stepped over it and entered the studio. It was morning. The studio was beginning to fill with a glassy winter brilliance. The room had a penetrating coldness to it because of an open window. There was also a faint smell of burned metal in the air. Autumn saw the blackened kettle on the window ledge. He closed the studio door and walked across the hardwood floor to the window. He removed the kettle, shut the window and listened for Kookla. The Mistress was waiting for him in the parking lot – he could hear Igor trying to restart the engine, but the studio was silent. He called for Kookla. There was no reply. Autumn sat down on the couch and raised a nimbus of swirling dust particles from the cushions. It felt like he had been gone for much more than twenty-four hours.

He'd have to wait for Kookla. He decided that she hadn't been gone for long because the burnt kettle was still warm to the touch. She must have wrapped up the smoke detectors to prevent them going off, then left. Autumn fell sideways onto the couch and lay there with his head on the armrest.

He didn't want to think about the possibility that she wouldn't come back. Autumn searched the studio for a distraction. He watched Attila swim around in the fish tank. He listened to a scraping noise from underneath the chesterfield. Luigi was gnawing his incisors on the chesterfield's wooden leg. Autumn flattened an ear against the upholstery – he could hear the monotonous grinding sound pervade the layers of foamy stuffing. Something in the chesterfield dug into his side, so he rolled away from the point, assuming that it was a jagged spring. It turned out to be a book. A journal, lost deep inside the cushions.

Autumn had never seen the journal before. He opened it to a waxy yellow paper near the back. It was an old circus popcorn wrapper. The paper's buttery surface was decorated with a lion's face and covered with writing. The writing continued from the wrapper onto the final pages of the journal. It wasn't Kookla's handwriting. Autumn started reading.

'Kookla suggested that we visit the circus. This was just before my expulsion from the medical program. It was a bad time for both of us. The relationship was wearing us down and we needed some cheering up.'

It was Robin's journal, Autumn realized. He knew that he should stop reading, but Igor's warnings about Robin made him continue.

'The morning of the outing was chilly and it had rained the night before. We walked around the circus grounds on the muddy grass trying to decide on a sideshow. Kookla didn't want to see the Anomalies of Nature exhibit. She said that freak shows are depressing. Along the way I bought myself some popcorn and Kookla cotton candy. She likes to eat her cotton candy off the cone so as not to make her fingers sticky. After only a few bites, she had grown a little pink beard, so I kissed her on the chin and tasted the spun sugar. Then it suddenly started to rain.

'People were running all over the circus grounds looking for shelter. Kookla and I ran into the nearest available sideshow. It was a magic act. The tarpaulin was decorated with symbols of the occult, like stars and crescent moons and floating eyeballs. A man with a flip of grey hair on his scalp greeted us at the entrance and sold us tickets. To my surprise, the inside of the tent was quite dry, almost dusty, except for the four other patrons who sat dripping on rickety wooden chairs. A fifth man, who was dry, was recumbent in his seat and snoring. The doorman's companion, a dowdy-faced woman, ushered us to our seats at the foot of the stage.

'The stage, a few packing flats held together with canvas, was only a few inches away from our heels. We could hear the rain overhead gushing down even harder. The fabric ceiling of the tent, with its colourful strings of electrical lights, strained under the weight of the storm. A thunderclap sounded and awakened the snoring man. He bolted upright in his chair and started clapping. He was soon back to sleep.

'The performance began without any fanfare. The man from the entrance, the ticket dispenser, stepped onto the stage. He was much older than I had first thought. His tuxedo, which must have been tailored for him years ago, made his body look thin and frail. It had been worn to the stitching at the hems and the oval sleeves. His body seemed to move inside the suit without ever touching the material.

'He conjured up a bounty of playing cards into the flats of both hands using a technique called the back-palm. This type of magic, I whispered to Kookla, was classic sleight of hand. It would never sell in the larger venues because of the lack of bulky apparatus and spectacle. These types of tricks were intended for the salons where a proximity to the audience was necessary. Unfortunately for the performer, it consigned the work to a sideshow where the turnouts and the earnings were less substantial. The elderly magician, nevertheless, was a pleasure to watch. He had performed this act so many times that he appeared to be disassociated from the manipulations. The effects were just as much a part of his physiology as breathing in air or filtering blood through his kidneys.

'Following a standard silver-dollar-over-the-knuckles bit, he addressed the sullen audience. "Ladies and gentlemen," he started. "This is the story of the lady contortionist and her ill-fated romance with the cannonball man." His voice was well tenored. It carried with it a sad reminiscence of earlier shows conducted in larger venues. "Her brother, the fire-eater, was unhappy with the affair." A pair of sewing thimbles appeared on his thumbs. "Although he had warned them to stop, they stayed true to their love." With a snap of his fingers the thimbles disappeared. The magician mopped his sweaty brow with a handkerchief. "Just so you know," he explained, "the big wooden cannon is a very difficult apparatus to install. It has to be fired three times before every performance." He folded the handkerchief into a little white bird with flapping wings. The bird nested quietly on the top of his right wrist. "The first shot is reserved for the cloth dummy. It weighs the same as the cannonball man and wherever it lands marks the bull's eye." The handkerchief bird suddenly reappeared on the magician's left wrist. "The bull's eye is drawn on the earth with a garden hose so it can evaporate after the net is set up." The handkerchief bird flapped its way back to his right wrist. "The second shot confirms the trajectory. And then, with the third shot, if the dummy lands on the net it's a go." The bird disappeared. The magician searched for the handkerchief, which had somehow returned to his breast pocket. Only Kookla and I and one other person applauded.

"'For my next trick," he announced, "I am going to prepare you all a delicious home-cooked meal." The magician gestured toward stage left, where his assistant, the usher, now wearing high heels and a tiara, stepped onto the platform. The uneven footing of the rostrum made her puffy ankles tremble. Even so, she graced the stage with an engaging smile and a large metal cooking pot. The pot, she happily demonstrated to the audience, was empty.

'The magician greeted his assistant warmly, then stepped to the back of the stage and produced a wooden gentleman's caddy. He positioned the caddy beside him as he started to undress. The magician kicked off his shoes, then unbuttoned his jacket and carefully draped it over the shoulders of the caddy. He stuck his thumbs underneath the elastic of his suspenders. "The fourth shot," he continued, "is set for the cannonball man." He snapped off the suspenders and let his pants fall to the floor. When he climbed out of his pant legs the audience could see that he was wearing a pair of black stockings held in place by calf garters. He brushed the pants flat and suspended them from a hanger on the caddy. The magician undid his bow tie and stuffed it into the pocket of his hanging jacket. He then worked at the buttons of his dress shirt, starting with the collar, and then the cuffs, and then the buttons from the top down to the bottom. He slipped out of the tuxedo shirt, placed it on a hanger, and added it to the caddy.

The magician stood on the stage in his underwear. His boxer shorts were decorated with the same mystical symbols as on the outside tarpaulin. Kookla covered her mouth and laughed. Suddenly, from behind his back, the magician produced a large head of cabbage. He chucked it into the cooking pot held by the assistant. Potatoes, celery, radishes and onions – everything went into the cooking pot. It was a wonderful trick – we unknowingly watched as he constructed a blind with the caddy from which the vegetables could be procured.

'"The cannonball man missed the net by a mile," he said as he stood there in his boxer shorts. "He crashed into the cheap seats like a meteor. We all ran over to the crater in the planks to see if he was dead. His girlfriend, the contortionist, was the first one to find him. She told me that his body was so tangled up that even she couldn't reproduce the position." The magician tapped a finger against his temple. "I'm forgetting something important," he added, "a special ingredient."

'While the magician was stirring his cooking pot, Kookla jumped up from her seat and shouted, "Oh … oh … oh!" From underneath her shirt appeared a small black rabbit. The magician applauded her. The audience applauded her. She held up the rabbit for everyone to see. She seemed to be genuinely surprised.

'"Anyhow," concluded the Magician. "I reckon that her brother must have stuffed the garden hose into the dummy's sawdust guts, making it heavier and screwing up the trajectory. That's why the cannonball man overshot the net. Unfortunately, by the time I had this all figured out, everything had dried up and the circus was gone. There was no evidence left to support my theory." The magician bowed and we all applauded.

'After the show I approached the magician. I wanted to buy the rabbit as a present for Kookla. He was reluctant to sell it at first, but then agreed. He overcharged me considerably. I should have known better. It was just another part of the performance.

A good old-fashioned grift. With me, the reliable boyfriend, singled out as the mark.

'As we were leaving the tent Kookla addressed the magician. She wanted to know the name of the cannonball man. He said that his name was Luigi.'

Autumn put the journal aside. He looked under the chesterfield and met eyes with the upside-down rabbit. 'You're probably hungry,' he said. 'That's why you're nibbling on the furniture.' Autumn fed Luigi a handful of lettuce. He then walked over to the aquarium. 'You must be hungry, too,' he said to Attila. He removed a container from the shelf and shook a five-dollar bill into his hand. Autumn looked at the bill. He had mistaken the bus ride container for the fish food. He searched between the cushions of his memories, trying to remember the last time that he and Kookla played a bus ride. It was a long time ago – money in the container meant that she had recently played with someone else.

Autumn stuffed the bill into his pocket and searched the studio for a note. He was hoping that Kookla, and maybe even the mysterious passenger, were waiting for him elsewhere. Unfortunately, there wasn't any note to be found. There was, however, a large tattered envelope on the floor with a telephone number on it. The overturned clock flickered 6:05 a.m. Autumn picked up the telephone receiver and called the number.

III

'Number … number …' Kookla's eyes swept the apartment directory like the pendulum of a metronome, from number to name and back again. 'Here it is,' she said, her finger on the buzzer next to Robin's name. She removed her stocking cap and mittens. Her hands were cold, so she shook them out and let the blood rush into her fingertips.

Autumn had left her the night before and now she was in the lobby of Robin's apartment. It had been more than a year since she and Robin had spoken. Kookla stood there and stared at the buzzer. She was thinking about Duffer's accusations – that she depended on others, that she lacked direction. He was sometimes a jerk, but he could also be extremely perceptive and unusually caring. And it was Duffer who had introduced her to Autumn, whom he had met at the university when Duffer was a poor theatre student who worked as a nude model for the Fine Arts department.

Duffer's apartment at the time had been on the ground floor of a three-storey complex. It contained a bathroom, a single bed and a desk with a lamp. A chair for the desk was beside a curtained window. When Kookla arrived at the apartment she saw a young man leaning against the desk. He was leafing through one of Duffer's texts on Stanislavsky. His shirt cuffs were dusted with charcoal. Duffer was cradling an armful of laundry. He stopped gathering clothes and gestured at Autumn.

'That's Autumn,' he said. 'I know him from the life-modelling class at the university.'

'Hello,' she said, 'my name's Kookla.'

'Hello,' said Autumn. He smiled and brushed self-consciously at his sleeves.

'Would either of you like something to drink?' asked Duffer as he opened up a closet door and revealed a small growling refrigerator.

'No thanks,' replied Kookla. She sat down on the bed. On the covers beside her was a large black portfolio.

Duffer dumped the laundry on top of the fridge and shut the door. He then sat down on a chair. 'Man, am I tired,' he said.

'Is the modelling strenuous?' asked Autumn.

'It is, actually.'

'Autumn,' she asked, 'is this your portfolio?'

'Yes it is, but it's only sketches.'

'Mind if I take a look?'

'Please, be my guest.'

Kookla removed several pages of newsprint from the portfolio. She looked at the drawings, then at Duffer. 'These are beautiful,' she said. 'They look just like you, Duffer.'

'He's a very good model,' said Autumn. 'It must be hard to model nude. I know that I couldn't do it. Not because I would be embarrassed – it has more to do with projecting self-assurance and confidence.' Duffer swivelled uncertainly in his seat. Autumn laughed. 'I'd probably look like a naked man directing traffic.'

'You never know,' permitted Duffer. 'Sometimes it's just a matter of finding a familiar pose.'

'There is something familiar about your poses,' considered Autumn. 'I'm certain that I've seen some of the gestures before.'

'You may have – they're all borrowed from an anatomy text-book. I find that representing the figures as a model is very much like acting.'

'Can I borrow that textbook when you're done with it?'

'Borrow it now.' Duffer straightened in his chair and pointed at the book on his desk. It was titled *De Humani Corporis Fabrica*.

Autumn looked at the book. 'Hey, I know this artist,' he smiled. 'This is Vesalius. He's on our reading list for Art History. How did you find this?'

'I got it from a friend.'

'Who?'

'A guy I worked with, a musician … '

'My last boyfriend,' allowed Kookla.

'Why would he have a volume of anatomic illustrations from the 1500s?'

'He was a doctor.'

'A doctor and a musician?'

'Well … a student doctor. Robin is also a classically trained musician. He knew about a composer, I think his name was Davies, who had written a set of fourteen dances based on these illustrations. Anyhow, Robin was thinking of remounting the production.'

'Did it happen?'

'It was going to, until he played me a recording of the *Vesalii Icones*, the musical composition.'

'And?'

'And … it was complicated.'

'You didn't like it.'

'Not exactly,' answered Duffer. 'I couldn't make sense of it. That's why I suggested we collaborate on something else.'

'Robin must have been disappointed.'

'He, uh, abandoned the production.' Duffer looked at Kookla. Her fingertips had blackened from handling the charcoal drawings. She would not look up from the portfolio.

'Autumn,' she said, 'pass me the anatomy text.' Kookla wiped her hands on her pants and reached for the book. She then placed it on her lap and flipped through the pages. 'I don't see any resemblance to the illustrations.'

'Look here,' said Autumn. He joined Kookla on the bed and helped her sort through the drawings. 'Do you see Duffer's pose here in the fourth plate of muscles?'

She compared the two figures. The text showed a man with raw musculature strolling in profile on the grass. 'They're identical.'

'Here, too,' pointed Autumn as he turned a page.

'Why is this figure supporting himself against a wall?' asked Kookla.

'It's because he's dead. Vesalius had to use cadavers for his models. He also used actors.'

Duffer leaned his back against the chair and watched Autumn and Kookla in silence.

'Autopsy was illegal during the Renaissance,' Autumn explained. 'It was considered a desecration of the body and therefore an act against God. Nevertheless, Vesalius and his students attended Venetian funerals, exhumed the corpses and studied the dead bodies in secret. It took many years of petitioning before a sympathetic judge finally allowed Vesalius the remains of executed male criminals. Still, there were very few subjects to render. As a provision, he preserved a few of the dead bodies in his bedroom. That's why some of figures in the book are inclined against a wall or suspended by ropes.'

'That's horrible,' squirmed Kookla.

'Vesalius reproduced, for the first time in history, a fairly accurate physiology. The drawings were engraved as woodblocks. The original woodblocks, three hundred of them altogether, were first struck by a printer in the mid-1500s. They were lost for almost four hundred years and then rediscovered in 1932 in the library of the University of Munich.'

'Where are the woodblocks now?' asked Kookla.

'They're gone.'

'Gone missing?'

'No,' said Autumn. 'The woodblocks were destroyed in the bombing of Munich during the Second World War.'

'What about the actors?' asked Duffer. 'How did they work with Vesalius?'

'The actors were hired as medical patients and models.'

'As patients?' said Kookla.

'They would undergo a physical examination. For example, he was very interested in the principle of nerve conduction.' Autumn pressed on the outside of Kookla's left elbow. Her funny bone tingled and she jumped away laughing. 'You see that?' he grinned. 'Vesalius understood that some kind of energy was responsible for the movement of muscles. However, in the sixteenth century, there was no understanding of electricity or neurotransmitters. So he decided to call this invisible force the Animal Spirit. He believed that the Animal Spirit travelled through the tissues of the body like a wind. A map of these winds are marked down here in Greek letters.'

Kookla massaged her singing elbow. She liked Autumn. He was cheerful and easy to get along with. While Autumn discussed the Greek letters and their indices, she moved in a little closer.

'Are you a full-time student?' she asked.

'No, only part-time,' he said. 'I also work in a second-hand bookstore. I'm usually there evenings and weekends.'

'It sounds like nice work.'

'It is nice work,' he said. 'A little dusty perhaps … '

Kookla smiled.

'My favourite part of the job is sorting through the new shipments. I'm responsible for inspecting the books before they go on sale. Sometimes I'll find something hidden in boxes or forgotten between the pages.'

'Have you found anything interesting?' asked Kookla.

'Lots,' he said. 'Foreign currencies, personal letters, photographs, and, my favourite, a pair of discarded library books.'

'Are they valuable?' she asked.

'No, it's just that one of the borrowers, a kid from the seventh grade according to the lending stamp, he drew pictures all over the books.'

'Did he ruin them?'

'I don't think so. His pictures related to the stories. He actually turned the novels into flip-books – you know, where the pictures move when you flip the pages.'

'What were the books?' asked Duffer.

'One is *Treasure Island*. It had a dancing skeleton brandishing a cutlass.'

'And the second book?' asked Kookla.

'*Moby Dick* – it had a whale surging out of the text and spouting water.' Autumn loved telling this story, but he was more interested in learning about Kookla. 'Are you a student?' he asked her.

'No,' she said. 'I'm an auto mechanic. I work in a garage with a friend, but I'm thinking of leaving. I might do some contract work at a general service station. Transmission jobs and wheel alignments – stuff like that.'

'She doesn't trust her boss,' Duffer said.

Kookla closed the cover of the anatomy text. She kept her eyes on Duffer. 'I trust Igor … ' she said. The end of the sentence was drowning somewhere between her and Duffer.

Duffer suddenly glanced at his watch. 'I gotta go,' he announced.

'What do you mean you gotta go?' asked Kookla. 'I thought we were invited to an opening.'

'We are,' he said, 'and Autumn, too, but first I have to look after something.'

'What?' she demanded.

'It'll only take a few minutes,' he promised. 'Just wait for me here and I'll be right back.' Duffer left the apartment.

'I'm sorry,' Kookla said to Autumn. 'He's trying to get us alone.'

'He is?'

She nodded. 'Duffer would never admit to this, but his falling-out with Robin, it was more than just a disagreement over a play – it was something more personal. That's why he's introduced us, he's trying to prove to me that his friendship is genuine. That it isn't … '

'That it isn't more than just a friendship.'

'That's right.'

'Well, there's no harm in our meeting, and as far as I'm concerned there's still a good chance that we can attend this theatre opening.'

'Without Duffer?'

'Yes, he asked me to hold the tickets. Would you still be interested in going?'

'Saddle up,' she said, 'we're out of here. But first I'm going to see if I can find him, even though he doesn't deserve to go.'

Kookla searched for Duffer at the building's entrance and mailboxes. She called out his name in the stairwells and inspected the area around the service elevator. She also tried the basement laundry room. It smelled like hot bleach, and the oscillating washers made a furious noise.

She found Duffer sitting on a chair. He was facing away from her and chewing a stick of gum. He rolled a piece of silver foil into a ball and dropped it on the floor. A man dressed in work clothes appeared. It was the building superintendent. He stood over Duffer and pointed at the floor. Duffer leaned forward and picked up the gum wrapper. The superintendent walked to the end of the room, grabbed a chair and dragged it back over to Duffer. At first he didn't say anything, he just sat in his chair and stared at Duffer. Then he started to talk; Kookla couldn't make out the words but his gestures were obvious. They had something to do with money, anger, a key and, in all likelihood, a dispute over the rent. Throughout all of this Duffer continued chewing his gum, but his hands moved unconsciously toward his groin.

He sat there covering his genitals as if they were a frightened bird that might fly away. The superintendent moved in closer until he was close enough to Duffer that their knees touched.

Kookla shook herself free of the memory. She looked at the directory and realized that the pressure of the tip of one finger on the buzzer was all that separated her from Robin. The space in between them was less than a quarter of a centimetre of connecting wire.

It was about eight in the morning. The nearby factory that shadowed Robin's building had just started production, flavouring the air with the smell of chocolate. Kookla imagined herself standing at the intercom speaking to Robin. She didn't know for certain if he would open the door or just leave her stranded on the soggy entranceway carpet. Her eyes returned to the list of residents. She avoided Robin's name and pressed on several different buzzers all at once. A garble of voices emanated from the intercom speaker. Kookla repeated 'Paperboy … paperboy … ' until somebody buzzed her inside. She then walked up the stairs to Robin's floor, pushed open the door, and entered the hallway. In the centre of the hall carpet was a pair of boots. They were placed one beside the other with the laces undone. As she walked around them on the way to the apartment she wondered if she, like the owner of the boots, was about to experience a sudden absence of gravity.

He gravitated toward the door, checking his pockets to make certain that he was prepared for the audition. 'Keys, wallet, headshots … ' When he opened the door Kookla was standing in the threshold.

'Duffer?'

'What are you doing here?' he stammered.

'I'm looking for Robin … '

'Robin isn't here. Now, if you'll excuse me, I have to get to my audition.' Duffer tried to move around Kookla but she blocked the doorway.

'Wait a minute,' she said. 'Where's Robin?'

'He isn't here,' said Duffer.

Kookla pushed her way into the apartment. She searched the individual rooms and called for Robin while Duffer waited anxiously by the door. Kookla finally sat down on the chesterfield. She crossed her arms and stared voraciously at Duffer.

'What are you doing here?' she asked.

Duffer's chin dropped down to his chest. He knew that he was in trouble. He glanced at his wristwatch. It was eight a.m. He could still make it to the audition for nine. He stepped back inside the apartment and closed the door.

'Do you remember my last apartment?' he asked.

'Yes,' answered Kookla.

'It's where you and Autumn first met.'

'Yes,' she repeated impatiently.

'Let's just say that I had to get out of there.'

'But this is Robin's apartment – his name's on the directory.'

'I lived here with Robin for a short while, around the same time that you and Autumn moved in together. It wasn't easy for me to ask him – we hadn't spoken from the time he left the theatre company.'

'What happened?'

'He was actually happy to see me. I told him I needed a place to stay temporarily, and he offered me the apartment. He also asked me to look after the place while he was away.'

'Where was he going?'

'He told me he needed to find somebody.'

'Who?'

'He didn't say.'

'So where is Robin now?' she asked.

'I don't know.'

'Duffer,' she cautioned, 'I don't believe you.'

'Believe what you want,' he said. Duffer opened the door and made ready to leave. Kookla got up from the chesterfield and caught him by the elbow.

'Tell me where he is,' she said.

'Why do you want to find him?'

'It's none of your business.'

'Do you still care about him?'

'Of course I do, you idiot!'

'Well, you're mistaken if you think that he still cares about you. I told him about your relationship with Autumn, I told him that you were happy and managing even better without him, even though he probably suspected I was lying.'

Kookla took a swipe at Duffer. He avoided the blow but stumbled sideways onto the floor. Kookla fell on top of him. She struggled with him and tried to secure his arms by the wrists. Duffer wrestled her onto her back and reversed the manoeuvre. She was unable to break his grip. When she tried to scream Duffer held a sweaty hand over her mouth. Kookla couldn't breathe.

Suddenly Duffer was gone. Kookla felt disoriented. She lifted herself into a sitting position on the floor. For some reason the crashing sounds of a struggle continued. Kookla wavered unsteadily into the next room. She found a male figure shouldering Duffer into a corner. Kookla was unable to see the man's face but she recognized the voice immediately.

'Stop it, Duffer!' shouted Robin. 'It's over now … settle down!'

Duffer tore himself away from Robin. He stood in the middle of the bedroom floor dishevelled and out of breath. He tried to straighten his clothing but soon gave up and sat down vacantly on the bed.

'What is going on here?' asked Robin.

Kookla wiped her nose against the back of her hand. Her nose was sore but it wasn't bleeding. Duffer spat on the floor.

'I'm going to my audition,' he said, 'so fuck you both, do whatever you want.'

'Not so fast,' demanded Kookla. She looked away from Duffer and faced Robin. 'And you … ' she said. 'You walk out on me and change your address, and all this time Duffer had to keep it a secret?'

'Kookla,' he said, 'I've come back here to be with you.'

'How did you know that I was here?'

'I knew you were here,' explained Robin, 'because of Duffer's signature on your doorstep.'

Kookla gaped at Duffer. 'What signature?'

Duffer simply raised a hand and shook his head.

'Answer me, Duffer,' she said.

Duffer rested on the edge of the bed with his head bowed forward and his elbows digging into his knees. 'You shouldn't be angry,' he advised.

Kookla was silent. She could tell that Duffer was preparing something terrible.

'It isn't like you haven't been keeping secrets … '

'Duffer,' she murmured.

'Robin,' he started, 'did Kookla ever tell you about the clothespins?'

Kookla closed her eyes and steadied herself against the door-frame. Robin didn't answer.

'I remember Kookla telling me about the clothespins,' Duffer said. 'Then again, unlike you, I never abandoned Kookla.'

'You know that's not true.' Robin was speaking now to Kookla instead of Duffer. 'I was preparing … '

'One time,' began Duffer, 'when Kookla was only eight or nine years old, she had forgotten to hang up all the washing on the clothesline.'

'Duffer,' she said, 'this is not for you to talk about.'

'Her punishment was to stand on the laundry basket undressed, her entire body prickling with clothespins. The wooden pegs were on her eyelids, on her nipples, pinching her lips and her labia together, on the tips of every finger … '

'That's enough,' said Robin.

'That's nothing compared to why she ran away from home.'

The telephone rang. It made Duffer start. He looked over at the small bedside table. The telephone rang a second time. Duffer was addled by the call. Robin, who was closest to the phone, lifted the receiver.

'Hello,' said Robin. He listened to the caller. 'I don't understand what you're saying. Who are you calling for?' There was a pause and then he hung up the telephone. He looked over at Duffer.

'That was somebody calling for the Ice Cream Man.'

Duffer shrugged his shoulders.

Kookla struck her hand against the doorframe. 'It's a telephone sex line!'

Duffer glanced at his watch.

'My good friend the actor,' she jeered. 'Promoting his craft on the telephone.'

'It's nothing,' reassured Duffer, 'just money … '

'What else are you doing for money?' she asked.

'Kookla,' he said, 'would it surprise you to know that I've done much more than just phone sex for money?'

Duffer raised himself from the bed. He buttoned his overcoat and brushed the carpeting from his shoulders. Kookla walked over to the bed and stood directly in front of him. She tucked in his shirt collar and straightened his hair. The tension abated. Kookla tried to look into his eyes but Duffer turned his face to the side.

'I don't think that I'll be seeing you again,' her voice trembled. 'But before I go, there's something that I want to share with you, and it's important that you know what I had to come through in order to share this with you.'

Duffer's lips tightened. He avoided Kookla's eyes. 'Please,' he said softly, 'don't go with Robin.'

'This happened early in the morning – an hour, maybe two, before sunrise. I was running away from the farmhouse in my nightshirt. My only chance of getting away was to run to the nearest train station six miles to the east. I had to scramble over gravel roads and wooden fences in the dark. When I finally arrived at the train station my feet were bloodied and swollen. My nightshirt was in tatters and I was covered with thistles. My plan was to board an open boxcar. I knew that this was dangerous because a member of the railroad crew, or even another traveller, might find me out and beat me for trespassing. In either case it seemed to me less frightening than dealing with my father.

'I limped across the stockyard searching for a place to hide. A southbound train was stopped beside a water tower. I made my way toward it and I saw an open freight car. It made me feel uneasy – I was worried that it might be a decoy. A man with a lantern suddenly appeared. I slumped down behind a guardrail and nervously picked at the briars in my hair. After a while I looked over the guardrail. The man with the lantern was in the distance. He was holding the lantern at knee level so that he could inspect the carriages for signs of metal fatigue and stress fractures. Once he was finished with his inspection he signaled the conductor with a whistle. The train pulled away. I hopped onto the open boxcar. The compartment was empty and I fell asleep.

'A man with a flashlight discovered me at the next station. He dragged me out of the boxcar and hauled me over to the conductor. The conductor listened impatiently as the man shouted and pushed at me. The conversation ended when the conductor tapped on his pocket watch. After the man with the flashlight rambled off, the conductor gave me a once-over. He then placed a gentle hand on my shoulder and guided me onto the engine. We entered the control room. I remember there was an instrument panel, some lockers and a swivel chair. There were rectangular windows surrounding the inside of the engine. I wanted to look out a window but they were too high above my head. The conductor addressed a few of the knobs on the instrument panel and the train began to move. He then walked over to the locker where a pair of blue coveralls was hanging. He handed them over to me and busied himself elsewhere. They were much too big for me, but I changed into them. They're still too big for me but I like to wear them when I'm working.

'Within a few minutes I was dozing again in the chair beside the conductor. As I lapsed in and out of wakefulness, the conductor placed his hands underneath my arms. I didn't know what he was doing at first but I didn't resist when he lifted me from the seat and carried me over to the front window. He held me there, close enough to the glass that my breath hazed its surface. At first I couldn't see anything, and then I noticed something illuminated by the light. There was a flickering object ahead of the train. It was an animal – a wolf. Its ears were pointed backwards and its legs were pumping madly. The wolf was racing over the tracks and steadily drawing closer to the engine. The conductor explained to me that wolves often scavenge the tracks. When a train appears they become frightened and run away. However, in their panic, they don't have the sense to run outside of the rails.'

Duffer quietly met eyes with Kookla.

'When I think about this wolf,' said Kookla, 'I think about you.'

Duffer nodded his head and tendered a smile. He then stepped in between Kookla and Robin and left the apartment. The last thing he heard as he walked from the apartment was the sound of the telephone ringing.

'Ringing the bell on the cash register is so uncool,' Monkeyblood mumbled to himself. 'But I can't wait around for the waitress all day.' He decided to ring the bell one last time.

The waitress appeared. She was holding a hand mirror and checking her front teeth for streaks of lipstick. Monkeyblood held up two fingers indicating breakfast special number two, buttermilk pancakes, no sausage. The waitress nodded ruefully and slipped back into the kitchen.

He decided to sit in a diner booth facing the entrance – a seat that overlooked the front counter, the bouncing red bar stools and the cash register. His braces were hurting this morning. The pancakes, he figured, were the softest thing on the menu. After a few minutes of sitting idle he removed a napkin from the dispenser and began scratching at it with a mechanical pencil. He was hoping that Kookla's friend Autumn would arrive soon.

Monkeyblood scribbled a musical staff on the paper. He worked on the bars for about ten minutes, thoughtfully dotting each measure with musical notes. Suddenly, an unexpected hand lighted on his shoulder. Monkeyblood looked up from the table and saw an unfamiliar face.

'Hello,' said Autumn. 'You must be Monkeyblood. We spoke on the phone.'

Monkeyblood extended a hand. 'Good morning,' he smiled.

Autumn shook his hand and stared at his teeth.

'You've noticed my braces.'

'I'm sorry,' he apologized, 'I didn't mean to stare.'

'Don't worry about it,' said Monkeyblood. He settled back into the booth. 'I've been wearing these braces for over ten years. My teeth are corrected – I just can't afford to get the braces off.'

Autumn sat down. 'I'd like to thank you for accepting my call and agreeing to meet with me.'

'Are you hungry?' asked Monkeyblood.

Autumn shook his head. He glanced quickly out the front window to where Igor sat, smoking, in the Mistress.

'I hope you don't mind if I eat something. That is, if the waitress ever shows up. I think she's in the kitchen fixing her face.' He gestured for Autumn to move in a little closer. 'By the looks of things,' he whispered, 'it might take a while.'

Autumn covered his eyes with his hands. The waitress was standing directly behind Monkeyblood.

'Would you like to order something?' she asked.

'Nothing for me,' replied Autumn. He couldn't bring himself to look at the waitress.

'I'll have a coffee with those pancakes,' winked Monkeyblood.

The waitress made a cursory note on her bill pad and walked away.

'I'd double-check that breakfast if I were you,' suggested Autumn.

Monkeyblood's eyebrows jerked upwards.

'All kidding aside,' said Autumn, 'I want to talk to you about Robin. I'd like to know where I can find him.'

'First,' asked Monkeyblood, 'how did you get my telephone number?'

'I thought it was Robin's number.'

'It used to be Robin's number. Did you get it from Kookla?'

'Indirectly.'

'You are friends with Kookla, right?' He decided not to mention her phone call.

'I am friends with Kookla.'

'Is that how you know Robin?'

'I don't know Robin.'

'I don't understand,' said Monkeyblood. 'If you don't know Robin, why do you want to find him?'

'I want to talk to him about Kookla.'

'Why don't you just talk to Kookla?'

'Because Kookla won't talk to me.'

Monkeyblood drummed his pencil on the table. 'I thought you and Kookla were friends.'

'There are certain things that Kookla won't talk to me about,' he specified.

'I see. And that's why you want to talk with Robin.'

Autumn nodded his head.

Monkeyblood had directed Kookla to the building opposite the chocolate factory. If Autumn wanted to find Robin alone, and speak with him about Kookla, he would have to take his chances elsewhere.

'He might be up at the cabin,' he said.

'Is it far from here?' questioned Autumn.

Monkeyblood paused for a moment and looked at the Coat Check Diner's cash register. It was a nickel–plated National with clacking metal buttons, drum roll calculations and a money drawer that rang *ka-ching*. It would have added nicely to Robin's collection of forgotten sounds.

'Yeah,' he replied, 'it's far from here.'

'Could you take me there?' asked Autumn.

'I can't,' he said. 'I have to be at a gig in about an hour, and you never know, Robin might not even be up there.'

'Why don't we just call him?'

'You can't – there's no telephone. It's a wood cabin on the outskirts of a milling town.'

'Where is this place?'

'Up north,' said Monkeyblood. 'A two- or three-hour drive in good weather.'

'You've got to be joking.'

'I'm not,' he said.

'Why there?'

Monkeyblood massaged his upper gum with an index finger. 'If you haven't seen Robin around lately, and he isn't with Kookla, then he probably wants to be left alone. That's why I think he's at the old cabin. We used to vacation up there once a year with my Uncle Louis. My Uncle Louis was a distiller.'

'What did he distill?'

'This goes way back,' chuckled Monkeyblood. 'Robin and I were twelve years old at the time. Uncle Louis was a part-time violin instructor. He was also a member of a travelling chamber ensemble. His touring schedule kept him fairly busy most of the year except for the last two weeks in September, when he would drive us up north. There, in the forest, we would help him distill chestnut whiskey. I remember the first time that we saw his equipment. It was after a long and arduous hike through the woods. The still was hidden in a clearing underneath a burlap cover. The copper body of the still was a pot rather than a column, in order to enhance the whiskey's flavour. The pot was about the same height as my Uncle Louis. It had four bandy legs and a long corkscrew tail. I told my Uncle Louis that his still looked like a monkey. He smiled at me and uncorked a silver flask. "Howard, my boy," he said, "come over here and take a nip." I tipped back the flask, which was warm from riding on my uncle's hip all day. The liquor was strong – so strong, in fact, it knocked me down onto the ground. My uncle picked me up and patted me on the back. Both he and Robin were laughing. "What is that stuff?" I asked. I was coughing out the words and fanning my tongue with a hand. "It's monkey blood," he said to me, and it stuck as my nickname from that moment on.'

'So that's where the cabin is,' reasoned Autumn, 'at the site of the still.'

'Not exactly. I haven't gotten to the cabin part yet. We learned that my Uncle Louis was distilling a high grade of liquor made from roasted chestnuts. Robin and I were responsible for collecting the chestnuts. Uncle Louis took care of the distilling. It began with roasting and mashing the chestnuts, then they're cooked for several hours in a bath of boiling well water and malt. Enzymes in the malt convert the starches in the chestnuts to fermentable sugars. The mixture is then combined with yeast and cooled. Yeast transforms the sugars into alcohol. Once the fermentation is complete, the mixture is ready for the still.

Inside the still, more heat is applied and an alcohol vapour is produced. The evaporated alcohol rises to the top of the pot, enters a condenser, which is the coiled monkey's tail, and reduces back into liquid. The droplets of alcohol are collected in a bottle and then emptied back into the still so that the process can be repeated with the distilled solution. This creates an extremely refined and incredibly potent blend of chestnut whiskey. Robin and I would sit around the campfire peeling the porcupine skins off the chestnuts while Uncle Louis sampled the products. By the end of the second run he was usually pretty soused.

'In the evenings, we would sit beside the smouldering fire, shell and eat the roasted chestnuts, and listen to my Uncle Louis play the violin and sing to us. The copper still, with its drunken breath, would whistle and hiss in the background like a calliope.'

'What about the cabin?' said Autumn. He looked out at Igor, who appeared to be asleep, a cigarette still hanging from his lip.

'The cabin will only make sense if I tell you about the conkers.'

'The conkers?'

'The chestnuts,' explained Monkeyblood. 'Robin and I would search for chestnuts in the morning, when the light was good. We would collect as many as we could carry in the fabric shoulder bags that my uncle provided. By the early afternoon we'd be back at the camp. We'd sort the gathered chestnuts into piles: a good pile for distilling and a bad pile for disposal. From the good pile we'd each select one chestnut for a game of conkers.'

'How do you play conkers?'

'I'd tie a string around my chestnut and swing it hard against Robin's chestnut. Then Robin would do the same. The winning chestnut would be played indefinitely, so long as it didn't break. The loser has to find another chestnut. We'd play this game for hours, with Robin constantly winning and me losing.'

'Was Robin cheating?'

'No, he wasn't cheating,' said Monkeyblood. 'Robin just had a good chestnut.'

'How does this tie in with his whereabouts?'

'It's like this … Robin refused to get rid of the winning chestnut. He always kept it safely tucked away inside a chest of drawers until the yearly excursion with my Uncle Louis. But one year my uncle's touring schedule changed, which meant that we would only have one more season up at the still. We were saddened by the news. Robin decided he wanted to retire the conker. This surprised me because the winning conker, over the years, had become his favourite keepsake. Nevertheless, Robin tearfully buried it in a break in the trees far removed from the still.

'We ended up going back a year later. My Uncle Louis had managed to find a replacement violinist for the two-week distilling period. Unfortunately, the weather was terrible. We were unprepared for the days and nights of freezing rain. Robin and I were eager to build up a campfire, but my Uncle Louis was opposed to the idea. The smoke, he informed us, would alert the locals to our activities – he was already nervous about the small amounts of smoke and steam produced by the still. So, instead, we had to warm ourselves by working hard. The unseasonable chill penetrated every soggy layer of our clothing. Our bodies were steaming in the cold as we gathered up chestnuts. The weather got worse, and in the middle of our chestnut collecting the persistent drizzle became a downpour. Robin and I decided to call it quits. We dumped out our chestnuts and forged our way back to the campsite. It was getting colder and darker. The clouds turned the colour of dirty mop water. Thunder was bursting around us and lightning lashed at the treetops. We searched and searched but couldn't find the campsite. I tried calling out for my Uncle Louis but there was no answer. Meanwhile, Robin kept on guiding us deeper into the forest. He was hoping to find some shelter in the denser brush, but it only slowed us down. The trees gathered around us like pickpockets. Then all of a sudden we heard a loud banging. We struggled our way through a path in the branches toward the sound. It led us to a small cabin – its wooden door was swinging open and closed in the wind.

'We entered the cabin as the storm pulled at the door. Water and lightning poured in through the cracks in the timber. We spent the night there, dripping wet and shivering on the cabin's dirt floor. In the morning, when I awakened, the door was open and Robin was standing outside. He was covered with mud. I had leaves in my hair and dirt under my fingernails. When I joined Robin he told me that he recognized the location. He also told me that the cabin, which had never been there before, was made entirely of chestnut wood.'

'And the location,' Autumn said, 'was the clearing where you had buried the conker.'

Breakfast arrived. There was a stack of three pancakes and a regular coffee. The waitress returned with a bottle of table syrup. She refused to make eye contact with Monkeyblood.

'To this day I don't know how to explain the chestnut cabin. A part of me wants to believe that it sprouted from Robin's conker. The news of the cabin frightened away my Uncle Louis – as far as he was concerned, it belonged to the local authorities. Anyhow, it ended our careers as distillers.'

'Draw me a map,' said Autumn.

'You won't find it,' warned Monkeyblood. He sketched on the back of his napkin with the pencil. 'You'll have to follow the access road north out of town. After the access road stops, you walk about a quarter mile east to a fence. Hop over the fence, enter the woods and continue east through the trees. There should be a trail there. I don't know if you'll be able to find it if there's snow.'

'Do you honestly think that Robin's up there?'

'I can't say for certain,' admitted Monkeyblood. 'But I can't think of anywhere else he might be.'

Autumn accepted the napkin. 'Enjoy your breakfast,' he said.

Monkeyblood called out 'Good luck' as Autumn left the diner. The clock on the wall read a quarter to nine. He had about fifteen minutes to finish his breakfast. He regretted flirting with the waitress – it had obviously affected the service. He drew a tentative sip from the coffee mug. The coffee tasted fine. He picked up the cutlery and examined the three pancakes. They appeared normal. He divided the stack in the same way a demolitions expert might uncap a landmine. The first nervous mouthful tasted good. He added a suspicious helping of brown table syrup. The second mouthful of pancakes tasted even better. He happily acquiesced and enjoyed the food. The short stack of pancakes finished quickly. After the meal, Monkeyblood wiped his mouth and leaned back into the vinyl seat of the diner's booth. It was only after he tossed back the last drops of his coffee that he noticed a funny aftertaste. Monkeyblood looked into the bottom of the coffee mug. Looking right back at him, with a black mascara wink, was a woman's artificial eyelash.

'Eyelash on your cheekbone,' said Duffer. He touched the actor's face with a pointed finger.

'Do you mind?' The actor stood up and moved to another seat.

'Hey, no hard feelings.' Duffer blew on the tip of his index finger.

Duffer understood that auditions are sometimes won from the green room. The reason he had decided to sit next to this particular actor, and bother him, was that he was an identical 'type.' Duffer's type, according to one casting director, was 'moody.' Which wasn't a bad thing – he just didn't want another moody actor to have a better audition. The other six actors, young men identical in age and appearance, sat on their fold-out chairs oblivious to the confrontation.

An actor near the entrance suddenly took notice of Duffer. He straightened in his chair and caught Duffer's eye. Duffer, anticipating an unfriendly glare, looked out the window. When he looked back again the actor was out of his seat and walking toward him. He sat down beside him and started talking.

'It's nice to see you again, Duffer,' he said.

Duffer studied the actor's face. 'Larry?' he finally remembered.

'That's right,' he nodded.

'Wow,' remarked Duffer, 'I haven't seen you in almost two years.'

'If not longer,' agreed Larry. 'The last time we worked together was on your production of *The Lust of the White Serpent*. Do you remember that show?'

'Don't remind me.'

'You know,' he said, 'none of us in the company really understood why the whole thing fell apart. I think it had something to do with the music director leaving, and then our stage manager … What was her name again?'

'You mean Kookla?'

'Yeah, Kookla. She left immediately after.'

'It was a big mess,' recalled Duffer.

'Have you seen either of them around lately?'

'No, I haven't,' lied Duffer.

'That's too bad. How about the other members of the cast?'

'Not a one,' answered Duffer.

'I've run into a couple of them,' said Larry.

'Like who?'

'Like Victor, for example. But this was a while ago. When he was C.T.D.'

'C.T.D.?' asked Duffer.

'Circling The Drain. He was giving up on his acting. He hadn't been working for a long time, so he finally had to accept a few menial jobs. His last job was driving a cargo truck, which ended with his arrest for possession of stolen property.'

'What?' exclaimed Duffer. 'Victor is a thief?'

'No, no,' quieted Larry. 'He was set up from the start. Get this. Victor was hired to deliver a van filled with stereo equipment. The drop-off was an electronics store, after hours, so as not to interfere with the regular business of the day. He arrives at the address, rolls open the delivery door and drives into the loading bay. The place is completely deserted. After unloading the equipment Victor starts up the van. He tries to leave but now the van won't fit through the door.'

'Why not?'

'Because removing the equipment lightened the load,' explained Larry, 'which raised the van's roof above the door lintel. He tries letting some of the air out of the tires but that isn't good enough. The van is still too high. So Victor decides to reload the van, park it on the other side of the door, and carry the equipment back inside. The minute that Victor drives the loaded van through the doorway he's arrested by the cops.'

'I don't believe it.'

'It's true. He's caught red-handed with stolen goods. Victor got six months. It could have been eighteen months except it was his first offence.'

'Who set him up?' asked Duffer.

'Nobody knows. I heard about it through his wife, Anne.'

'How is she doing?'

'Not so good. She's fed up with Victor, and she has to contend with the new baby whom she lovingly refers to as El Diablo.'

Duffer smiled. He remembered that Anne was a much stronger actor than Victor. It was likely that she had retired from acting in order to look after the baby. Their situation saddened

Duffer. Nevertheless, it was nice to talk with Larry. The conversation helped to relieve some of his pre-audition tension. Larry seemed to appreciate it as well. He and Duffer settled back into their seats like vacationing tourists on a pair of sunny deck chairs.

'How are things going for you?' asked Duffer.

'Not bad,' answered Larry. 'Not bad at all. I was in a couple of good shows.'

'What were they?'

'*Sixteen American Dragons* … '

It sounded unfamiliar.

'*The Slow-Motion Smokers* … '

Duffer shook his head.

'I'm not surprised you haven't heard of them. They were short runs. Sort of like the shows you used to organize. I'm sorry that you missed them.'

'I'm sorry, too,' responded Duffer.

'I still can't figure out how you were able to afford the costs of our theatre rentals,' ventured Larry. 'We had impressive productions, don't get me wrong, but the returns from the box office … they were less than spectacular. How did you manage it?'

Duffer shrugged his shoulders. 'It must have been the grants,' he attempted.

Larry put the question aside. 'And how are things for you?'

'Hand to mouth,' he said. 'When things get bad I model nude at the university.'

'I was thinking about doing that,' considered Larry. 'How is the money?'

'Pretty good, but I have to subsidize it with another university job.'

'What's that?'

Duffer hesitated. 'Working as a standardized patient for the medical students.'

'Now that sounds really awful,' shuddered Larry.

'It isn't what you think,' said Duffer. 'Sure, there's some poking and prodding. But most of the time it's just answering questions.'

'No probing?'

'No probing.'

They shared a quiet laugh.

'Do you want to hear my audition piece?' asked Larry.

'Sure,' replied Duffer.

'I'm not going to run through the whole thing,' he said. 'Just what the piece is about.'

'That's fine with me.'

Larry cleared his throat. 'This goes back to a time when I was a kid at the zoo with my father. He was a tall man and he let me ride on his shoulders all day long. It made me feel like a giant. It was an old zoo. Many of the cages were overcrowded and the animals were constantly begging us for food. We noticed that some of the cages had signs posted on them saying that the zoo was about to be closed. The animals, we learned, were to be transferred to other facilities.

'By the end of the day we arrived at the polar bear cage. We watched the bear circle the stained floor of his pen with a grey, expressionless face. My father lifted me from his shoulders and set me on the ground. His attention was drawn to a newspaper article mounted on the bear's cage. It read that the polar bear was the zoo's first and oldest inhabitant. He had been acquired as a cub and had lived his entire life inside the same small cage. Because of his age, instead of being sent to another zoo, he was going to be returned to the Arctic. My father and I were both heartened by the news. The word "Arctic," he told me, comes from the Latin word "Arcticus," which means Constellation of the Bear. We waved goodbye to the polar bear and wished him a safe journey home. It was a wonderful end to our day.'

'Is that the end of your piece?' asked Duffer.

'No,' said Larry. 'A few months later my father called me into the TV room. A news report concerning the polar bear's release was on the set. I clambered onto my father's lap and watched the telecast. A team of animal handlers, wearing fur-lined parkas, released the polar bear onto a shimmering patch of ice. At first he just stood in one place and blinked. After a little while he started walking. The bear walked in repetitive circles as if he were still confined to his old cage.'

Duffer considered the audition piece carefully. 'That's a good monologue.'

'Thanks,' replied Larry. 'I was worried that it might be too personal.'

'I don't think so,' reflected Duffer.

'It was a bit of a rush job,' said Larry, 'on account of the announcement.'

'What announcement?'

'Oh yeah,' mentioned Larry. 'You weren't here for the announcement.'

'What announcement?' Duffer blanched.

'Before you arrived, an agent announced a change in the audition criteria. They're now suggesting a monologue based on a family experience.'

'Are you certain?' asked Duffer.

'Absolutely.'

The door to the green room opened and a man with a number-one haircut entered. He was flipping through the pages on a clipboard. 'Mr Lawrence Able,' he requested.

Larry stood up from his seat. He brushed the creases from his trousers and smiled at Duffer. 'Wish me luck,' he said.

Larry and the man with the clipboard exited the green room.

'Jesus Christ,' thought Duffer, 'I'm screwed.' He had stumbled unexpectedly into what might have been one of his own devices. He felt ashamed for doubting Larry, who had always been a decent friend and a reliable colleague, but he also felt overwhelmed by the dilemma. Duffer nibbled on a thumbnail and considered asking one of the other actors in the green room about the announcement, but he was too embarrassed. A family experience would have to be based on his mother. Duffer crouched forward in his seat and wrapped his hands around the back of his head. To the other actors in the room he resembled a man preparing for a crash landing.

The landing for the bus terminal steps had not been shovelled. Robin trudged across the snowy platform with a cup of hot coffee in each hand and entered the station. He found Kookla sitting by herself at the far end of a row of seats. He handed her a cup.

'This is for you,' he said, 'but be careful, it's hot.'

Kookla took off her mittens and enjoyed the warmth of the foam cup before drinking. She didn't say a word to Robin.

Robin sat down beside her and quietly finished drinking his coffee. He looked over at Kookla. She was watching a man clean the receivers on the public telephones.

'The coffee from across the street is much better than what they serve here,' he said.

'Robin,' she said, 'what are we doing here?'

'Here, at the bus terminal?'

'No, I mean why are we here together, you and me?'

Robin pursed his lips and shook his head. 'It's been a couple of years and I thought maybe, after all this time, I could just talk with you and see how you're doing.'

The overhead PA system shouted a series of chartered arrivals. People in the bus terminal stopped talking or walking and stared up at the ceiling until the announcements had finished. The ceiling clocks read 8:51 a.m. and the station was bustling with commuters.

'I've wanted to speak with you, but that was before,' she said.

'I can only imagine … '

'Can you really?' she asked. 'I remember waking up, Robin, thinking you had gone to work, and by evening, when you hadn't come home, I knew that something was wrong. I called the hospital and your friends, and they were surprised to hear my concern – they told me that you were fine and that everything was normal. For some unexplained reason, on that morning almost two years ago, you decided to suddenly shed me and our life together like a worthless skin.'

'I am so sorry,' he apologized.

'You moved out without telling me. I also learned from Duffer that you composed a score for his Japanese play and never once throughout the production attempted to speak with me. Finally, the only time I got a chance to see you was in the hospital, after you had almost died from alcohol poisoning.'

'You have no idea how important that was to me.'

'After our talk in the hospital, I thought, because of your expulsion from the medical program, we could be together. I thought maybe you might need me, and I could forgive you, and we could resume our relationship – and once again you disappeared.' Kookla blew the steam from her coffee cup and took a drink. 'It was even harder for me the second time.'

'I was hoping you might let me explain.'

'While I was sitting here, waiting for you to return with our coffees, I thought, what if he doesn't come back? Then, a familiar anger started to well inside me again. I tried to remember what I had said to you in the past, the words I had wanted you to hear. But I couldn't remember them – all I could think about was how you look thinner, and that your hair is a little longer … '

Robin placed his empty cup on the floor beneath his seat. He desperately wanted to touch her, to kiss the curve of her collarbone, to caress the contours of her lips. Instead, he put his hands in his pockets and accidentally touched the plastic bag.

'I was afraid you would come to harm if we stayed together.'

'If you mean the cutting,' she said, 'that's been going on for a long time. That had nothing to do with you.'

'No, I mean something much worse, something I would regret doing.'

'Is there something you'd regret more than leaving me?'

'Yes.'

'What?'

Robin shook his head. 'I needed time away from you to consider alternatives.'

'Where did you go?' she asked. 'How come I couldn't find you?'

'When I first left our apartment I lived in the music studio. I slept underneath my piano for almost three months. After I lost my position at the hospital and my senior resident's pay, I had to move again. Monkeyblood took the studio and I took a smaller apartment. From that time on I worked as a health-care aide in a nursing home. I did overnight shifts, so I never really had to stay in my apartment. By the time Duffer moved in I had already moved out. We'd overlap once in a while and Duffer would tell me about you … ' Robin paused for a moment. 'About you and Autumn.'

'What did he tell you?'

'He told me you were happy.'

Kookla finished her coffee and put the cup on the floor.

'Do you love Autumn?' he asked.

'Yes,' she replied without hesitation, 'I love him. I was hoping that one day you might see us together. Autumn would be holding me and I would be smiling at him and you would be standing there watching. I held onto this wish, that you were somehow watching us, until you haunted my thoughts like a ghost. You became a third person in our relationship, and Autumn, who had never known you, he began to feel your presence.'

'Where is Autumn now?'

'I don't know.'

'Do you know if Autumn loves you?'

'He told me that he loves me.'

'Could you be happy with Autumn?'

Kookla covered her face with a hand. Her green eye was hidden from Robin, but her blue eye was bare and its lashes were wet. 'No,' she said.

Robin tenderly, nervously, lighted a hand onto Kookla's cheek. She touched his hand, held it uncertainly, and slowly accepted its warmth. He could feel her quiet sobbing. Robin's eyes were burning with tears; he pinched his eyelids shut, trying to swallow them down. He allowed his forehead to shore against Kookla's neck. She burrowed a hand into his hair and drew him in closer. They sat in the terminal holding onto each other. It recalled Kookla's photographs: a couple embracing, motionless, amid a background of blurring rush-hour travellers. Robin asked her a question.

'Why does your hair smell like smoke?'

Kookla pulled back, smiled and wiped the tears from her eyes. 'I burned the kettle.' Her expression immediately sobered. 'Robin, ' she asked, 'what happens now?'

'I want you to meet somebody.'

'Who?'

'It's the only person who can help us.'

'If it's another doctor,' she said, 'you can forget it. I'm not participating in any more therapies and I won't take medication. We've been through this before and you know as well as I do that nothing helps. I'll just have to slam on the brakes whenever an unexpected childhood memory throws me into a spin.'

'Yeah, but your habit of cutting was getting worse.'

Kookla fanned open her fingers and exposed the fresh cross-hatching of scars. 'It might have been worse,' she said, 'if Autumn hadn't stopped me.'

'I'm worried that you'll end up killing yourself.'

'I'm worried about that, too.'

Robin gazed directly into her eyes. 'There's still one last thing we haven't tried, but it won't be easy – in fact, it will be the hardest thing you'll ever have to do in your life.'

'What is it?'

Robin thought about his second option, the one he was concealing from her, and it made him afraid. 'Kookla,' he said, 'you have to see your father.'

Kookla sat motionless and stared at Robin.

'I contacted your mother by phone a few months ago. She told me that your father wasn't well. I was surprised to learn, after I had visited your home, that he was no longer living there. Your mother wouldn't tell me where he'd gone. One of her farm workers, however, told me that he'd suffered a stroke. I figured that he must have been admitted to a convalescent home.'

'You saw my mother?' Kookla pulled on her fingers.

'Yes, and I found your father by accessing the nursing-home placement service. He's been admitted to a medium-care floor in a residence not far from the farm.'

'Did you see him?' she asked quietly.

'No,' he said. 'We can see him together.'

'Oh my god,' she trembled. 'What have you done?'

'You have to do this,' urged Robin. He grasped her hands firmly and tried to untangle the knotted fingers. 'There's no other way.'

'Let go of me!' she said. Kookla stood up from the seat and struggled with her mittens. Her eyes searched the terminal for an exit.

'Please, Kookla,' he pleaded, 'just sit down and think it over.'

She didn't move. Her body, however, was in full flight, with pumping heart, shortened breath and dilated pupils. Robin stood up and gently guided her hands into the mittens. He then sat back down and waited for her to make a decision. Kookla's heart rate slowed and her breathing returned to normal. She sat down on her seat, testing it gradually as if she were entering a tub of boiling water.

'Thinking about seeing my father,' she said, out of breath, 'it makes me sick with fear.'

'You shouldn't be afraid. There's nothing he can do to hurt you. He's just an old man in a retirement home.'

Kookla's eyes were downcast. 'It doesn't matter.'

'What doesn't matter?'

'Seeing my father again, if anything, it'll only make matters worse.'

'How?'

'I've survived up till now by escaping my father. If I should see him again, and stir through the cinders, I'll start to remember things that I shouldn't.'

'But that's all a part of getting better,' he said.

'No it isn't, because whenever I remember something bad it makes me weaker, closer to really hurting myself. One day, when I'm better, I'll tell you why I had to run away from home. It's one of the only things that I can remember. After that you can ask me again about visiting my father.'

Robin sank into his seat. He dipped his head between his legs.

'Are you all right?' she asked.

'Yes,' he said. 'I'm fine – tired, that's all, and out of ideas.'

'Is there nothing left for us to do?'

'I think there is,' Robin said, recovering, 'but we need some time alone.'

'All right.'

'Good,' he said, his expression brightening somewhat. 'I know a quiet place where we can go.'

'Where is it?'

'It's a cabin up north.' His stomach churned its contents like the drum of a washing machine. 'That's why I brought you here to the station.'

'You look ashen,' she said. Kookla touched his forehead.

Robin stood up. He took off his glasses and wiped his face. 'I'll be right back.'

'Where are you going?'

'Tickets,' he said, pointing at the counter.

'Don't take too long.'

Robin watched Kookla from his place in the line. She reached into a pocket of her jacket and removed a wool stocking cap, which she stretched down over her eyes and her ears. She then crossed her arms and eased her back into the seat. It looked like she was about to fall asleep. When it came to Robin's turn in line he approached the clerk and stated his destination.

She quickly checked the timetable. 'Your bus departs at three p.m.,' she said and handed him a schedule. 'How many passengers?'

'Two adults.'

'Return?' she asked.

'No,' he replied, 'one way.'

IV

'Way for us to travel,' said Igor, 'is more to east, no?'

'No,' replied Autumn. He checked the map again. 'Just keep driving straight until you reach the turnoff for Highway 11.'

Igor drove the Mistress over a snow-covered section of country highway. She wiggled her chassis with every sideways glide over black ice. They had travelled over two hours and more than half a pack of cigarettes from the city. There was at least another hour of steady driving ahead of them.

'Tell me again,' asked Igor, 'where are we going?'

'We're going to a cabin outside a small town.' He folded the road map. 'We may have to walk through the woods to get there.'

'You have not told me before of walking through woods,' complained Igor. He rolled open his window and held the tail of his cigarette in the wind. It sparked in the cold air and then pinwheeled away from his fingers. He closed the window and nodded at a pack on the dashboard. 'Please, to get me another cigarette.'

Autumn opened the pack. 'There's only one left.' He handed the cigarette to Igor.

Igor stuck it between his lips and pressed on the dashboard lighter. He then searched another pack underneath the driver's seat, above the sun visor and in the pockets of his oil-spattered parka.

'I must stop and get more smokes,' he said.

'We don't have the time.'

The car lighter clicked and Igor lit his cigarette. 'From when are we in a hurry?' he asked. 'Maybe Robin is not even there.'

'He might be,' said Autumn, 'and Kookla might be there with him.'

Igor steered the vehicle onto an exit ramp.

'What are you doing?' demanded Autumn.

'Look,' he said, 'at end of ramp is service station, they will have cigarettes.'

Autumn glanced at his watch – it was almost six. 'By the time we get up there it'll be dark and we won't find the cabin,' he said angrily.

'My friend,' relented Igor. 'Please to not be upset. Remember you are asking me to drive and I am driving with you for many hours to cabin. But now I am needing one pack of cigarettes. It is taking maybe one minute.'

'Please,' Autumn implored, 'let's do this quickly. We've already been delayed.'

'I could not leave garage any sooner,' Igor said, dashing the cigarette.

The Mistress left the exit ramp and approached the roadway. As she coasted down the slope toward the service station her engine stalled. She suddenly coughed, cleared her airway and resumed her pace as if she had recovered from a choking spell.

'What happened?' asked Autumn.

'It is nothing,' said Igor. He shifted the car into neutral and pumped on the gas pedal. The engine hesitated slightly with every spur of the accelerator.

'What is it?'

Igor balanced the cigarette between his fingers. 'It is maybe plugs,' he said and scratched an eyebrow. 'It is like hiccups for car, nothing serious – still, I must stop and check engine.'

He parked the Mistress several metres away from the service area. The complex consisted of a gas station, a restaurant and a parking lot with four cars.

Autumn looked worried. 'This is serious,' he said.

Igor zipped up his parka. 'I am turning off engine – there is maybe a chance it will not start again.' He switched off the transmission. 'Wait here … ' Igor opened the glove compartment and removed a rusted plug socket from the clutter.

Autumn could feel the car body twinge as Igor worked under the hood. He looked toward the service area and noticed several people, men and women, sitting in the restaurant. The men were all wearing hunting caps.

'I found problem,' said Igor as he climbed back in the car. 'Is spark plugs. Feh … city driving, it is stopping and starting all the time and making burning oil.' He held up one of the plugs. 'See, is here carbon buildup in firing point.'

'So, what do we do?'

Igor produced a thin metal file. He tapped it on the spark plug and smiled. 'I scrape and we go.'

'How long will this take?'

'Maybe for five minutes,' he replied. 'Explain to me again why such a hurry?'

'Because there's a problem.'

'With plugs there's no problem.' He gently filed away the corrosion.

'Not with the plugs,' said Autumn. 'There's something I didn't tell you.'

'What?' Igor blew smoke on the plug's air gap.

'Before, when you told me about the booze can and Robin and your tattoo, I became very frightened for Kookla.'

'It is Robin who is injured,' recalled Igor.

'Do you know why?'

'No.'

'It's because he threatened Kookla and a friend tried to protect her.'

'Who is this friend?'

'His name is Duffer. He's an actor, and he was working with Robin at the time of the Medicine Show.'

'How was she threatened?'

'It had something to do with Robin's last theatre production. He and Duffer were directing the production but they couldn't agree on the ending. It was a Japanese play called *Jasei No In*.'

'What does that mean?'

'*The Lust of the White Serpent*,' he translated. 'It's an old Japanese fable about a young scholar who encounters a woman who is more beautiful than a reflection of cherry blossoms on the water.'

'Kookla is not like cherry blossoms on water,' considered Igor. 'She is more like rainbow in puddle of gasoline.' He started filing down another dirty spark plug.

'They fall in love and the scholar learns that his beloved is an evil spirit. She's an ancient white serpent whose nature is governed by lust.'

'Lust, it is a word that means for wanting sex, no?'

'Yes, but it can also mean desire.'

'Desire for what?'

'For Kookla, it's a desire to forget her past. But she has no control over her memories. It's like she's survived a disaster and every so often a piece of the wreckage floats up to the surface.'

'What becomes of scholar?'

'He attempts to rid himself of the spirit but is unsuccessful. Finally, with the assistance of a holy man, he captures the spirit inside an iron pot.'

'What becomes of spirit?'

'She gets buried in a temple.'

'Is unhappy ending for a love story.'

'That's why Robin wanted to change the ending.'

'How is he to change ending?'

'Kookla told me that Robin wanted a traditional romantic ending.'

'What, that spirit and scholar are happy together?'

'No,' answered Autumn. 'A traditional romantic ending for a Japanese love story is a double suicide.'

Igor stopped working and looked up at Autumn. He then placed the tool in its kit and brushed the filings from his pants. 'I put back plugs and you start ignition.'

The Mistress started without any trouble. Igor stood outside the car and inhaled the last of his cigarette. He dropped the filter in the snow and listened to the engine.

'Come on,' shouted Autumn, 'let's go!'

Igor walked over to the passenger door. Autumn rolled open the window. 'Is not so good,' he told Autumn. 'Will get us there but I am not for certain will get us back.'

'It'll have to do.'

Igor was staring at the parking lot. 'The silver car near the restaurant,' he said, 'it is also six cylinders like the Mistress.'

'Igor, please, just get in the car … '

'I am swift,' he said. 'Watch – I am getting for us new spark plugs, and also cigarettes.'

'Don't do it,' said Autumn. 'We don't have the time and we can't fuck around with the people up here.'

'Swift,' he repeated.

Igor walked into the restaurant. Autumn shut the window and cursed. He sat there and watched as Igor greeted the counter staff, paid for his cigarettes, left the restaurant and lit up a smoke. He then watched Igor walk over to the silver car and open the hood. While he was busy removing the spark plugs three men appeared from the restaurant. They followed Igor to the parking lot.

Autumn beat his fists on the horn but it wasn't working. He got out of the car and started running. By the time he was halfway to the parking lot the local men had Igor on the ground. Autumn stopped running and stood in the snow breathing heavily. He looked up at the sky. The sun was beginning to set. He heard Igor calling his name.

Igor had asked him before if he loved Kookla. He had asked him if he was capable of doing something terrible in order to help her. Autumn hadn't answered. But now, as Igor lay face down in the snow with a man's knee crushing the back of his neck, he had an answer. Autumn turned away from his friend and ran back to the car.

'A car in the driveway overnight meant laundry in the morning … '

'Hold on a minute,' said the first assistant director. 'Duffer's monologue,' he announced, 'take one.'

'Ready,' prepared the director, 'and action.'

Duffer was sitting on a metal chair in the middle of a large room. A white fabric drop cloth was hanging from the ceiling behind him. Staring at him were the camera, lights and production crew. Duffer concentrated on the camera. He had declined the musical accompaniment in order to focus on his monologue. 'Take a break, Professor,' he said to the piano player. The director and crew responded with mild surprise to his request but no offence was taken, even by the accompanist, who sat complacently at his piano running a mucousy finger back and forth along his sore teeth and braces.

'My mother instructed me in the basics of laundry when I was about six years old,' Duffer began. 'I had to wash all of our clothes in the kitchen sink, wring them out and hang the wet clothes outside on the line. If my mother had a special dress somewhere in the pile it had to be washed separately and ironed.

'A special dress in the pile meant a "caller" was coming. I was never introduced to the callers but I would often see their cars in our yard late at night when I was supposed to be asleep. They were always gone by morning. Sometimes they would leave a ring of razor stubble in the sink or an extra dirty cup on the counter.

'One summer weekend, when I was still in my early teens, my mother approached me with a white dress in hand. It was a showy little number, cut low in the front with a blue floral pattern. She wanted it washed right away. So I filled up the sink with warm water, added detergent and soaked the white dress. While I was busy with the washing she nervously arranged small things in the other room.

'At a quarter to three in the afternoon my mother entered the kitchen and sat down on a chair. She smoked a cigarette as I wrung out the dress. At five minutes to three she told me to finish up. I handed her the dress and she inserted a wooden hanger between its shoulders like she was baiting a lure. She returned the dress to me and pointed at the clothesline, which was behind the cottage just a few minutes walk up a hill. Before I walked away she sprayed the dress with lavender perfume. She liked how her dresses smelled when the sun and the air dried the perfume into the fabric.

'I carried the dress up the hill to the twins, a pair of old maple trees with a laundry line tied between them. A few neglected hangers swayed and chimed along the cord. At the foot of the first maple tree was a chair, now on its side and desperately weathered. I had used the chair to reach the cord when I was younger. I jumped up with the dress and hooked its hanger on the line. The other hangers bucked and tossed like startled horses. It was a muggy afternoon and the breezes barely stirred the fading grasses beneath the trees. They caused the dress to shimmy seductively on the line.

'A buzzing noise passed through the air beside my ear. It was a honeybee. It scribbled around me for a little while until it lost interest and lighted onto the sleeve of the white dress. A few other honeybees appeared. They were attracted to the sweet lavender perfume of the dress and searched the blue printed flowers for pollen.

'The sound of a door slamming stole my attention away from the bees. I turned and looked down at the cottage. From my position on the hill I could see that there were two cars parked in the driveway. This was the first time I had ever seen a car, let alone two, parked on our property during the day. The first car was grey and the second brown. The brown car drove away, leaving the grey car and its driver behind.

'I walked down the hill to the cottage. I entered through the back door and its springs released a dog-yawning kind of sound. I could tell that the cottage was empty. There was, however, somebody sitting outside on the porch. I walked toward the front door and found a man sitting on the front steps. He held on his lap a jagged object covered with linen. The man didn't look at me. He simply smoothed out the creases of the linen with his right hand. The fingernails of his right hand, I noticed, were black.

'I recognized the man immediately. He was my science instructor. At first I wasn't sure what to feel. I decided to sit next to him on the steps. "Lightning can strike a man twice," he said. I flicked a mosquito off my knee and looked into his face. He stared after the brown car. The suit he was wearing was made from good fabric. His hat was white felt. It was apparent that he had dressed for the occasion. He continued to stare after the brown car. When it was gone he lowered his eyes to the parcel on his lap. It was a gift he had intended for my mother. A shallow sigh escaped his lips. He unbuttoned his collar and dragged loose the silk tie. "You want to see something?" he asked me. I nodded.

'He removed the cover of the parcel and revealed an arm's length of delicate branching. This branch was unlike any other natural branch I had ever seen before. It looked like it was made from ice. I touched an index finger to the nearest twig. It was warm to the touch – the same kind of warmth that a glass pendant holds when it's kept against the body. My science instructor attempted a smile. He told me that it wasn't a branch at all, that it was actually a root. A lightning root. What scientists call fulgurite. He had acquired it many years earlier.

'He went on to say that he had been working in the garden when it happened. He didn't remember the lightning strike but he remembered awakening on the ground with his clothes soaking wet. When he tried to sit upright a ringing in his ears made his head spin. He was eventually able to stand. The clothes on the right side of his body were singed but his skin underneath was untouched. The leather of his right shoe was split from ankle to heel. He untied the shoe and realized that his right fingernails and toenails had turned black. The ground underneath his right heel was smoking. That's where he discovered the lightning root.'

The first A.D. swept a hand across his neck, a signal to Duffer that his audition time had ended. Duffer acknowledged the gesture and concluded his monologue.

'My mother tried to leave me in the care of someone she trusted – my science instructor. A man who loved her very much, at least enough to make a present of a piece of lightning.'

Duffer felt exhausted. He didn't know for certain if he had in fact met the audition's requirements. Regardless, he anticipated the provisional 'We'll let you know if there's a callback tomorrow.' His muscles went to mush. Meanwhile, the production crew busily wrapped up his audition. The floor lights were switched off. The videotape was removed. After the clamour subsided, a clapping sound was heard. It was coming from the director. He was sitting upright in his chair and applauding. Duffer looked puzzled. The director stood up and intensified his applause. The other members of the production crew watched. And then, one by one, they all stopped their work and joined in the applause.

Duffer got up from his seat and smiled for his audience, but the smile was really for Kookla. She had always asked him to perform honestly. He was surprised to find that he could stop acting. This was a defining moment.

'A moment ago you were sleeping,' said Robin.

'No I wasn't,' replied Kookla.

'Yes you were, I heard your teeth grinding.'

Kookla rubbed her eyes and looked out the window. The sky was cloudy white, and the ground, except for the grey of the highway, was white with snow. Kookla drew a spiral on the frosted glass with a finger. She looked at the scabs on her hands.

'What time is it?' she asked.

'Almost five.'

'How much longer till we get there?'

'I'm not sure. The driver's agreed to stop the bus before it enters the town. He'll let us know when to get off.'

Kookla erased the watery outlines with the edge of her hand. A liquidy patch of white scenery trickled down the glass.

It was a quiet ride after that. The bus continued along its route, stopping in a different small town every twenty minutes or so. The towns were invariably the same: a barbershop, a grocery store, a gas station and a post office. In between them Robin would look over at Kookla. She seemed to sink a little bit deeper into the bus seat with every stop. By the limits of the third small town he finally said to her, 'Get some rest, I'll wake you up when we get there.'

'I'm not tired,' she said. 'I was just thinking.'

'What were you thinking about?'

'About our last night together, when you returned from the hospital and tried to undress quietly before coming to bed.'

'I thought you were asleep.'

'No, I was awake, and I watched you slip out of your shoes and your socks and your pants. I remember you putting your glasses on the bedside table, and you did it so carefully, it made me feel even more love for you. Then, when you stripped off your shirt, and your arms and your head were inside the material, I could see the static charges crackle around your body. I imagined that you were being created right there in front of me.'

'Do you know what I remember?'

'What?'

'That you smelled like fresh lemons.'

Kookla nodded and closed her eyes. She rested her head on his shoulder. It was only twelve hours ago that she and Duffer had first talked about Robin. He had claimed that Robin was in trouble and needed some help.

'Did you steal something from the hospital antiquary?' she asked abruptly.

'Who told you that?'

'Duffer.'

He answered reluctantly. 'Yes, I stole something.'

Kookla smiled. She figured the only thing that Robin would steal from the hospital was the sailboat charm, the one from the X-ray. The meaning of the gift swelled her heart.

'Won't you reconsider?' he asked.

'Reconsider what?'

Robin's voice sounded hopeful. 'A visit with your father.'

She turned away from him and touched a hand to her lips. 'I can't,' she said. 'Please don't ask me again.'

'Why?'

'Because it's over, it's behind me.'

'No, it isn't,' he said, touching the cuts on her fingers.

'I ran away from home because of my father,' she said. 'I'm not running back to him for help.'

'Why not?'

She stared out the window. The passing farmhouses dissolved into the whiteness of the horizon. 'I was a twin, you know.'

'What?'

'I had a twin brother, Amos, but he died shortly after we were born. My mother had complications with the delivery and required a hysterectomy. My father holds me responsible for this. He believes that I murdered his son and ruined his wife.'

'What Duffer had mentioned earlier about the clothespins,' recalled Robin, 'were all of your punishments so cruel?'

'Yes, and the punishments were always fitting. My father was strict with me and I had to behave. There was, however, one time I decided to disregard the rules.'

'What happened?'

'I was fourteen years old, and I was checking the line to the milk house for leaks when I heard a sound. I looked down at my feet and there, on a patch of straw, was a mother cat feeding her kittens. I dropped to the ground and covered the litter with straw. My father hated cats and buried them in a hole in the vegetable garden.'

'Where did they come from?'

'City boy … you can't avoid cats on a dairy farm. What surprised me most about the litter was its exposure. You'll find the moms or the toms on the prowl but the kittens are always kept in hiding. I sat there on my knees and uncovered the four tabbies. They were maybe two weeks old, because their eyes were still closed and they were nursing loudly. The mother was dead. The moment I realized this my father called for me. I gathered up the tabbies and covered the mother's body with straw. It was against my father's wishes to keep animals in the house. Regardless, I crept into our cellar with the kittens in my pockets and left them on a blanket near the furnace.

'I looked after the kittens for about a month, feeding them stolen cream with an eyedropper. Two of the kittens died but the other two survived. They kneaded on my feeding thumb with every meal, and after they finished nursing I would hug them both against my chest and feel them purr. It was a wonderful and frightening experience for me. I would sit on the cellar floor with the kittens on my lap and listen to the creaking footsteps of my father overhead. My plan was to release the kittens after they had been weaned.

'One day, of course, we were discovered. My father opened the cellar door, turned on the light and instructed me to bring the kittens upstairs. It happened just as I had imagined it would.'

'What did you do?'

'I did what I was told. I picked up the kittens and climbed up the steps. My father was waiting for us at the top. He was wearing a pair of overalls, a denim jacket and rubber boots. He stank of soured milk and perspiration. My mother was standing at the kitchen sink rinsing off our supper plates. Her face was turned away from us. It was the time after supper when my parents finished their chores and I went to bed.

'My father walked out from the house. I followed him wearing only my nightshirt and stockings. The sky had a soupy look to it. I remember that the temperature outside the farmhouse was cool but I could still feel the day's warmth on my feet. We were heading in the direction of the vegetable garden. One of the kittens was licking at my wrist. When we arrived at the garden my father walked up to hedgerow fence and pushed straight through. I must have stopped, not knowing what to do, because I remember him calling after me, "Come along now." I forced my way through the hedge.

'We were now outside of the vegetable garden in a field. The field was untilled and its grasses had grown above my waist. It was hard for me to walk because the grasses knotted around my legs and pulled me down. I could hear the crickets chirping and one of the cows lowing in the distance. But my father said nothing. I followed him closely for another half an hour. He suddenly stopped and moved to the right of his path. I could see that there was something ahead of him – it appeared to be a circle made of fieldstone.

'The stones were held together with mortar and the lines in the mortar were damp with green moss. My father turned around and looked at me. He then jerked a thumb at the stones to indicate that I should climb onto the structure. I managed to climb up with a kitten balanced on each arm. The kittens were squirming. The sky had turned black and the stars seemed to swell up. When I looked inside the circle I could also see the stars – it was their reflection on water. I suddenly realized that I was standing on the old well.

'My father spat into the well and wiped his mouth with the back of his hand. I didn't hear the drop but I could see the night sky ripple. I turned around and tried to jump onto the path but my father stopped me. He nodded his head at the well. I understood what he wanted me to do but I couldn't do it. I held on to the kittens. My father finally shook his head, grabbed one of the kittens by the scruff of the neck and dropped it into the well. After a few seconds of silence I heard the splash. I shut my eyes tight and hid the last kitten behind my back. We waited. This time my father spoke openly. "Do I have to watch you all the time?" he asked.

'I opened my eyes. My father was removing a leather satchel from his jacket pocket. The satchel opened in three parts, like a wallet, revealing a tangle of brown suture and two instruments. I recognized the equipment immediately. The first metal instrument was a blade with a hook on it for cutting the umbilical cords of newly born calves. The second instrument, a thick silver needle, was threaded with the suture material. It was used for sewing up the cows after birthing. I started to shiver. My father moved in closer. The stink from his clothing was so strong it coated my tongue.

'"Do I have to watch you all the time?" he repeated. He touched the curved blade against my gown and sliced a straight line from my chest down to my groin. He never touched my skin but the quickness of my breathing made me feel lightheaded. I had to struggle with my footing. Meanwhile, the kitten was worming around in my hands. My father moved in closer. With a hand on the fabric he started to sew my nightgown back up. At first he was gentle with his sewing. Then, gradually, as the mending got closer to my groin, he began to pull harder. He tugged on the suture and unbalanced me. I was about to fall into the well. All of a sudden I heard a splash. I looked at my hands in disbelief. The kitten was gone. I held my hands against my face and started sobbing. My fingers smelled faintly of the kittens. My father knotted the last stitch. He put the instruments away and pocketed the satchel. I continued to sob as he lifted me up from the well. "I know how to watch you," he whispered in my ear. He then set me down on the ground.'

'Did you run away after that?' asked Robin.

'No,' answered Kookla. 'I went to bed and fell asleep, and then something woke me up.'

'What was it?'

'A terrible noise from the barn. It was an animal in pain and its cries entered my open bedroom window. One of the cows, I figured, needed an extra milking. It happens sometimes. A cow will call out when her udders get swollen.

'I walked over to the barn in my bare feet. The noise was getting louder and it was coming from the back of the pen. Using a flashlight, I trudged my way between the restless Holsteins. I followed the sound of the lowing cow and found her standing in a corner. I held her in my light. She took in a deep breath and bellowed. I lumbered on toward her speaking softly, my feet sinking into the manure. Her bellowing continued.

'When I reached the cow I brushed her coat. It was damp with sweat. I crouched down beside her and touched her udder, but it felt empty. Then something dripped onto my cheek. It startled me. I touched a hand to my cheek and felt a tacky liquid. In the light of the flashlight I could see that it was blood. Another drop of blood ran down my shoulder. It trickled down my arm like molasses and painted a burgundy stripe from my elbow to my little finger.

'I scrambled to my feet. The beam of the flashlight sharpened against the cow's face. She was missing an eye. It had been carved out from the socket with a knife. The flashlight dropped onto the ground. I wrapped my hands around my belly and touched the thorny suture on my nightgown. I finally understood what my father intended. I knew what he wanted to do with the cow's eye in order to watch me. That's when I ran away from home. I ran out of the barn and I just kept on running.'

There was a long silence.

'How can you endure this?' Robin asked.

Kookla's smile was the bravest thing that Robin had ever seen.

'If you hadn't awakened … '

'It wasn't by accident.'

'What do you mean?'

'The window in my bedroom was opened,' she recalled. 'They're normally closed because of the flies and the smell of manure. It was a warning from my mother. She wanted me to leave the farm. I don't think there was any other way that she could protect me from my father.'

'Hey, buddy,' called a voice from the front of the bus.

The driver parked the bus and turned around in his seat. He called again. 'I'm talking to you, friend.'

Robin stuck his head into the centre of the aisle. He saw that the driver was leaning away from the wheel and looking in his direction.

'This is your stop,' he announced.

'We're here,' Robin said. Kookla didn't seem to understand. 'This is our stop.'

Kookla responded sluggishly. She supported herself between the rows of empty bus seats and followed Robin to the front of the vehicle.

'Cross over the highway to that fence on the left,' instructed the driver. 'And if you follow that fence, maybe about thirty metres or so, it'll lead you to the access road.'

Robin did up the buttons of his overcoat and looked through the windshield to the fence. He thanked the driver. Kookla was waiting for the coach door to open.

'It's going to get dark soon,' informed the driver. 'Wouldn't it be better if you stayed overnight in town and then travelled to the access road in the morning?'

Robin's forehead wrinkled. He glanced over at Kookla. She responded by moving in closer to the door.

'We'll be all right,' assured Robin. 'If there's any trouble we'll just head back into town.'

The driver pulled on the door lever. 'Suit yourself.'

The door opened wide and a freezing wind entered the bus. Robin and Kookla stepped down, landing ankle deep in crusty snow. It was colder outside than they had expected, and the sudden drop in temperature caused them both to shiver. Robin tried to warm himself by marching up and down in one spot, while Kookla clapped her hands against her upper arms. The door of the coach swivelled shut with a hydraulic wheeze. The driver, still visible through Robin's frosted eyeglasses, pointed a determined finger in the direction of the town. He then shifted the engine out of neutral and returned the bus to the highway. Robin and Kookla started walking through the snow.

Snow water pooled in the plastic boot tray outside Duffer's apartment. He'd squirmed out of his boots and positioned them normally, one beside the other, on the mat. For the first time in a long time, Duffer ignored the other boots in the corridor. He had decided never to bother with his neighbours' footwear again.

Duffer entered the apartment and closed the door, then took off his coat, emptied out his pockets and walked over to the couch. Standing in front of the couch he extended his arms and held his breath, like a cliff diver before the descent, then slowly fell backwards. When he landed on the cushions their stuffing bulged under his weight. He watched the swirling eddies of house dust crest over the pillows like a big foamy splash of water.

Duffer was in a good mood. He lay on the couch cheerfully recollecting the particulars of the audition. He could have continued with the monologue, describing in detail his experiences with the foster families. There had been four different families within a seven-year period. They each had their problems, and Duffer's place in each family felt like a walk-on role in a daytime serial. He learned that he could connect or disconnect with these people as he wanted.

Duffer honed this ability by enrolling in his high school's drama courses. He demonstrated a talent for acting and acquired the leading roles in the annual reviews. He earned the only scholarship available to a university applicant based on acting ability. The university was in the city – he couldn't wait to go.

He decided to pay a last visit to the cottage before he left. It had been more than seven years since he had last been there – or since he had last seen his mother. He wasn't exactly certain why he was going back, except that he wanted to say goodbye to something before leaving for university.

A taxi drove Duffer to the entrance of the property. The cab driver parked on the gravel shoulder. He cranked up the flag and stopped the meter. Duffer paid his fare and instructed the driver to return in one hour. He got out of the cab and walked a short distance to the gates, which were open. He folded his arms over the top of one gate and peered in. The stony footpath to the cottage was overgrown with summer grasses. He proceeded along the path, dispersing a fireworks display of brown grasshoppers with every step. They showered over his body, a few of them landing softly on his chest and shoulders.

When Duffer finally arrived at the cottage he was sweating and out of breath. He peeled off his sticking T-shirt and pushed it through a belt loop on his pants. It was almost noon and the sun was directly overhead. Nothing cast a shadow on the ground. The cottage, seven years after he had gone, had become faded and lifeless.

Duffer sat down on the cottage's front steps, where the shade from the balcony helped cool his skin. He began to pick at the briars and twitch grass that clung to his socks. While working at the prickles he noticed that the porch had been vandalized – curse words and pentagrams had been carved into the wood of the railings.

Duffer stood up and instinctively reached for the front door, but it was missing. When he entered the cottage it was musty inside. Only a few cracks of sunlight were admitted through a set of panelled window frames. He walked between several piles of refuse on the floor and accidentally kicked a beer bottle, which spun on its ribs like an injured rat. It made Duffer nervous – the wobbling noise from the bottle could have alerted someone in the cottage. He took in a deep breath and moved carefully forward. There was a vinegar smell that grew more acrid as he neared the central staircase. It was the smell of urine. His passage through the stagnant air swept it up from the corners.

When Duffer climbed the staircase he remembered to stop at the halfway mark and look down to his right. From his position on the stairs he could see into the kitchen. A waterfall of willow branches had poured in through a broken window. The branches swirled over the countertops, overflowed the metal sink and spilled onto the floor. The floor was mostly buried underneath a layer of red soil, the leafy debris which had decayed and accumulated over the years.

Duffer continued up the staircase. The graffiti on the walls became so dense and overlapping it obscured the underlying wallpaper. He stopped and inspected the spray-painted messages. Some of them had been dated, which provided a chronology of the cottage's infestation of party-goers and transients. The earliest date coincided with the year of Duffer's departure.

There were three rooms on the second floor: a washroom, a small storage room and Duffer's room. Duffer decided to visit his room first. The furniture was missing and the floor was littered with empty liquor bottles. A scratching sound emanated from behind a closet door. Duffer withdrew to a corner, where he was startled by a filthy mattress lying on its side like an unconscious derelict. On his way out, walking around a burn hole in the floorboards from a neglected cooking fire, he stepped on something hard. The object stuck into the rubber sole of his running shoe. He extracted it and held it between his thumb and index finger. It was a piece of black metal the size and shape of a tooth. Duffer examined it more carefully in the light of the window. The object, he remembered, was an electrical component from the radio receiver. He sighed and pitched it out the window. That's when he saw someone standing in the backyard. It appeared to be a woman.

Duffer ran from the cottage and charged up the hill. The woman's body occupied the centre of an amber haze. A bouquet of rising wildflowers blossomed at her feet. When he reached the plateau he suddenly stopped, recognizing the maple trees standing on either side of the woman.

He started laughing. The honeybees had colonized his mother's perfumed dress. A patch of the dress was still visible underneath the golden hexagons of the honeycomb. It had survived on the line all these years, but its weight had caused the line to curve down so that it was suspended only a few inches above the ground. Duffer walked away from the dress. He was afraid of disturbing its humming cordon of bees.

Duffer returned to the couch. He rested there thinking about his success with the audition and how he had wanted to share it with Kookla. But she was gone – he had spent the day looking for her. Duffer threw an arm over his eyes. He had never felt so tired. It was only six p.m. and he was falling asleep. He had fallen asleep on the same couch when it was Robin's apartment. The telephone rang in the other room. Duffer let it ring and then stop – he had no interest in speaking with any of his customers. And then he remembered the callback.

Backing up against a tree, coat sleeves catching on the branches, Autumn finally admitted that he was lost. He turned around and started walking in the opposite direction, but his footprints were difficult to retrace in the dark. He pressed on for another hour and stopped. There was no definite path anywhere. He rested with his hands on his knees and glared at the tracks. The foot-prints he was stepping in were larger than before. He suddenly realized that he was following someone else's tracks

Autumn lost all hope of finding the trail back to the access road. The tiredness and cold that he was feeling were over-whelming. He closed his eyes and let his body fall into the spiny thicket of the chestnut trees. The branches coddled him and daubed his shoulders with spoonfuls of snow. 'If I fall asleep now,' he said to himself, 'I'll probably die from exposure.'

He opened his eyes. There was a faint smell of smoke in the air. Autumn desperately searched the horizon. A wisp of dark smoke trickled up from the woods about half a mile away. Autumn looked again at the footprints in the snow. They seemed to lead toward the smoke.

When Autumn arrived at the wood cabin he placed a hand against the door. It was cold, but there was a discernible warmth coming from inside. Autumn pushed against the door but it was locked. He thumped on the door with his fist and waited.

The beam of a flashlight suddenly drilled into him.

'Turn around!' a voice instructed.

Autumn turned around. The flashlight blinded him.

'Keep your hands out in front of you!'

'Is that you, Robin?' asked Autumn.

'Shut up!' ordered the voice. 'How many are with you?'

'What?' responded Autumn.

'How many are in your party?'

'It's just me,' he answered. 'I'm alone.'

The circle of the flashlight started at Autumn's feet, then followed his footprints from the cabin to the woods, confirming there was only one set of tracks. 'Keep still,' said the voice. The flashlight searched the trees and returned to Autumn.

Autumn stared incautiously at the figure. He was a large man with a menacing silhouette. The only other feature that he could discern was a long black shotgun trained in his direction.

'Step away from the door,' he said.

Autumn stepped away from the door.

'Now turn to your left and walk to the front of the cabin.'

Autumn walked to the front of the cabin. The man with the shotgun was following closely behind. When they reached the front door, Autumn stopped and looked at the ground. There were footprints in the snow that slipped heel to wall around the timbered corner. The man with the shotgun had circled around him.

'Open the door and get in,' he said. The barrel of the shotgun touched Autumn's shoulder.

They entered the cabin. The sudden warmth and complete darkness of the cabin were stifling. They shrouded Autumn's face like a hood.

'Sit down on the floor,' the man said.

Autumn sat. The man with the shotgun locked the front door. He stood above Autumn with the flashlight.

'Who are you?' asked Autumn. He sat on the floor with one hand protecting his eyes from the light.

The man switched off the flashlight and plunged the cabin into complete darkness. Autumn could hear the sound of winter boots clomping on the wooden floor, mattress springs groaning and a match striking flint. The flame wavered steadily in the air, then floated gently toward an oil lamp where it ignited a wick. The man placed a glass chimney on the neck of the lamp, then adjusted the flame by rotating a small copper key. As the flame slowly brightened, a warm ripple of smoke emptied from the blackened spout. The darkness of the cabin diminished. The man blew out the match.

The man with the shotgun kicked off his boots and placed his wool-stockinged feet on the bed. He stared directly at Autumn. 'If you stay right where you are,' he said, 'I'll put down the gun.'

Autumn nodded.

The man locked the safety catch and placed the gun down. He was careful to keep it within reach. A box of shotgun shells were scattered on the floor near the fireplace. The ash in the fireplace was soaking wet and its embers were hissing. A small wooden pail was lying sideways on the floor. The water drops around the pail reflected the light of the oil lamp. The man had extinguished the fire when Autumn knocked on the door. He must have tried to load his gun in the dark.

The man was in his late fifties. His beard and his hair were red, and he was wearing long underwear that was open at the neck. A green military-style jacket was draped over his shoulders. The patches on his sleeves identified him as a forest ranger.

'Trespassing in this area could get you killed,' he said.

'You have no authority to shoot trespassers,' replied Autumn.

'Not me,' he corrected. 'The poachers. They sometimes take shots at people in the area. We lost a ranger to them a year ago. That's why I carry a gun and that's why you're lucky to be alive right now.'

'Who are they?'

'Who are you?' he asked.

'My name's Autumn. I'm looking for my friends, a man and a woman, maybe you've seen them?'

'What are they doing in my territory?'

'I think they're looking for a cabin, a chestnut-wood cabin.'

'What for?'

'I'm not sure, maybe they just want to be alone.'

'If they want to be alone,' he asked, 'why are you following them here?'

'I'm worried about the woman's safety.'

He scratched his beard. 'It's none of my business.'

'You must be familiar with the area?'

'I'm busy with the poachers.'

Autumn tried to engage the ranger. 'What are they poaching?' he asked.

'They're poaching bear ... I figure they're with the Asian market because the bodies are butchered of their heads and paws. The last forest ranger who was stationed up here, a friend of mine called Emmet, he was murdered the same way.'

'What do you mean?'

'The poachers cut off his head and his hands.'

Autumn sat on the floor and stared at the ranger.

'They mounted his body on a tree stump like he was a trophy on display. I identified the footprints of three different men. They circled and admired his remains. I later followed Emmet's footprints back to a cache of charred bones and grey ash.'

'I don't understand why they killed your friend.'

'They killed him because he incinerated their trophies with a gasoline fire. Unfortunately for him, the smoke alerted the poachers. They hunted poor Emmet for a long time, according to the coroner who examined his remains. The most incredible thing about Emmet's death,' considered the Ranger, 'was the message he left for his wife.'

'You spoke with her?'

'No, I attended Emmet's funeral. After the ceremony was over the coroner approached her and placed something small into her hands. The object, whatever it was, made Emmet's wife cry. When I went over to comfort her I noticed that she had two wedding rings on her finger.'

'The coroner gave her the second wedding ring.'

'That's right.'

'Was he affiliated with the poachers?' asked Autumn.

'No, he found the ring during the autopsy – it was in Emmet's stomach.'

'What was it doing there?'

'After three days of running from the poachers with no food, and no chance of escaping, he gave up. He knew they would catch him and kill him. He understood that his head and his hands would be cut off. He might even lose his skin. The only way that Emmet could let his wife know that he loved her, and that his last thoughts were about her, was to hide the wedding ring in a place where it wouldn't be stolen. That's why he swallowed the ring.'

'I'm sorry about your friend,' said Autumn. 'But I need to find my friends, and I need your help to find them.'

'I've seen their footprints,' he said. 'A man and a woman, walking close together, maybe even holding each other. They're heading in the direction of the chestnut cabin.'

'How far away is the cabin from here?' asked Autumn.

'Not far,' he said. 'It would only take a few minutes on the snowmobile.'

'Let's go, then.' Autumn stood up from the floor.

'Hold on a minute,' said the forest ranger. 'I'm not leaving here till morning.'

'This can't wait,' he said. 'We have to go now.'

The forest ranger yawned and rested back into his pillows. 'Forget it,' he said, buttoning the neck of his long underwear. 'Wait until morning.'

Autumn walked to the door. He unbolted the lock and looked back at the ranger. The ranger shook his head and tossed over the flashlight. 'Take this,' he said. Autumn caught it. 'Follow the treads of my snowmobile west for about thirty minutes.

It should take you directly to the chestnut cabin.' Autumn opened the door. 'One last thing before you go,' he said. 'Don't expect me to come looking for you when you get lost.'

'Lost another customer,' chuckled Duffer. He answered the telephone expecting a callback, but instead it was a regular caller. He insulted the caller and hung up the telephone. It was something that he had wanted to do for a long time.

Duffer realized that he would have to find another job. There was always the nude modelling and the standardized patient programs but the pay wasn't very good. There was also the possibility of working with another theatre company but that depended on the callback.

He returned to the couch and thought back to his original one-man theatre company. He had mounted the productions almost six years ago when he was still in university. The shows were always unique to their locations. An abandoned rendering plant set the stage for a tragedy, while the backyard swimming pool of a vacationing neighbour presented an island adventure. It was trespassing, which meant that Duffer's audiences had to be relatively small. However, the more people heard about him, the more people showed up. For his fifth secret show, a drama set underneath the expressway, more than a hundred people were expected. This is where he first met Kookla.

It had been late in October, when the sunlight diminished by one minute every day. Duffer scheduled the show for midnight, when the expressway would be quieter. There would also be fewer police cruisers on duty. On the night of the show he chalked a white chain of pointing arrows on the elephant legs of the underpass. The arrows led to a ring of upside-down milk cartons that defined the location of the performance. After sweeping the site Duffer looked at his watch. It was only eight o'clock and it was already dark. He looked overhead. The industrial bulbs of the underpass sputtered and diffused a weak film of blue light. He hadn't anticipated a problem with the lighting. The audience would have trouble seeing the performance. But he had an idea. There was a garage with a body shop near the on-ramp to the expressway.

Duffer rushed over to the garage. The sign on the office door read 'Closed,' but he heard a loud noise coming from the side of the building. He ran over and found one of the mechanics wearing blue coveralls and a cap. Duffer shouted 'Hello,' but the mechanic didn't answer. Instead the mechanic jumped up in the air, grabbed at the garage door, remained hanging there and then slowly carried the metal joints down to the ground. Duffer came up beside the mechanic. He noticed the name 'Kookla' written in black marker over the breast pocket.

'Hello,' he repeated.

She lifted the brim of her baseball cap and looked at him. 'We're closed,' she said.

Duffer hadn't expected a woman. He tried not to look surprised. 'Oh, right,' he said, 'but I really need some help.'

Kookla gave him a look. It said that she was tired and wanted to go home.

'Where's your car at?' she eventually asked.

'It's not my car,' he explained. 'I need some help with a play.'

Kookla walked away from Duffer. 'I can't help you there, pal.'

Duffer jogged beside her. 'Please,' he said, 'just look at this.' He handed her an invitation. Kookla stopped and read the piece of paper.

'I don't understand what you're doing here,' she said, returning the invitation.

'I'm doing a show at the underpass, but it's too dark, I need more lighting.'

'What makes you think that we've got lighting?'

'There's got to be something around here that I can borrow,' he said. Duffer looked over at the garage. He was holding onto Kookla by the arm. 'Does your garage have a portable generator?'

'We have a gasoline-powered generator,' she said. Kookla pulled her arm away from Duffer.

'That's fantastic!' replied Duffer.

'But it makes a lot of noise.'

'How much noise?'

'You've got to shout while it's running.'

'Damn it!' He desperately searched the garage and the car lot for an alternative. Kookla quietly watched him as he struggled.

'Are you really serious about this?' she asked.

'I am,' he said.

'Why?'

'Because I love acting. It's important to me.' He looked into Kookla's eyes and noticed that they were different colours. 'Isn't there something that you love to do more than anything else in the world?'

Kookla didn't have an answer.

'I'm sorry,' he apologized. 'That was a stupid question.' Duffer started back toward the underpass. 'Thanks anyhow.'

'Hold on a minute!' she called out. Duffer stopped and turned around. Kookla had removed a pair of leather work gloves from her back pocket. She tucked her hands into them and gestured for Duffer to follow her.

They walked to the rear of the body shop, where columns of wrecked cars and assembled car parts were sorted.

'How much time we got before the show?' asked Kookla.

Duffer checked his watch. 'About three hours.'

'That's plenty,' she smiled.

Kookla set to work. She jimmied the grill off a crushed rear-ender and salvaged the front headlights. She then crawled underneath the suspension of an old school bus and stripped away handfuls of wire cable. The third car wreck gulped Kookla down like an oyster as she attempted to recover its battery.

'Is there anything I can do to help?' offered Duffer.

'No,' echoed a voice from underneath a car hood.

Kookla tunnelled her way into several other vehicles. She removed their headlights, as well as their wires and batteries. It took her almost two hours. When she finished, she assembled the car parts into a series of eight battery-powered headlights. Kookla attached a jumper cable to the lead battery. The battery sparked, ignited the headlights and produced a searing white light with incredible deer-killing intensity. She took off her gloves and wiped the sweat from her face. Duffer wanted to kiss the speck of clean forehead between her oily eyebrows.

'I could fashion the headlights into a circle,' she suggested.

'That would be great,' he said. 'Thank you.'

Kookla spent a few minutes at the sink cutting the grease from her hands with a sectioned lemon. 'How far away is this place?' she asked.

'Not far,' answered Duffer. 'It's at the underpass.'

Kookla thought for a moment as she touched the back of her neck with a rag dipped in warm water. 'We can drive the lights over on the truck.'

Over two hundred people arrived for the performance. They sat together on blankets in groups of twos and threes and waited for the show to begin. A few people brought thermoses, others brought flasks or rolled joints. There was a lot of excited talk. The talking stopped at midnight when Duffer stepped into the circle of light.

Duffer waited patiently for the crowd to settle. The city chimed softly in the distance and maintained a sunken bell tone of sound. A car passed on the expressway and caused the whole structure to ring like a stemmed glass. The audience was ready. Duffer began his performance. He needed to connect with the crowd as a whole, but he also needed one person in the audience who could respond to and meter his performance. This evening, he decided, his barometer would be Kookla.

Kookla was seated near the front of the stage on a plastic milk crate. Her baseball cap brim was turned backwards. This was the first time that she had ever attended a live performance. She watched as Duffer prowled the circumference of the lights. It reminded her of a story about tiger hunting in India, how the hunters captured tigers by surrounding them with a curtain of silk. That's how Duffer moved – illuminated, striped with shadows. She and the others outside of the circle were transfixed.

When the play finally ended Duffer left the stage. He exited the ring of lights into silence. The audience stood up from their seats and applauded. Duffer returned and graciously bowed, thanking the audience for their attendance. It took another twenty minutes or so for the audience to disperse. People stayed to congratulate him, and a few other actors wanted to discuss acting techniques and the possibility of working together. By the end of it all, Duffer was exhausted. Still, he wanted to find Kookla to thank her again for her help.

By this time, however, Kookla and the pickup truck had gone. All that remained of the performance was a circle of dimming car lights and some overturned milk cartons. Duffer wandered the performance site. Its emptiness made him feel even more alone. He looked again at the car lights and noticed something in the middle of the ring. It was Kookla's baseball cap. He couldn't believe his eyes. Inside it was money, at least a couple hundred dollars in bills. Kookla, without mentioning it, had 'passed the hat.'

The money from the one-man show, and the other performances stage managed by Kookla, created Duffer's theatre company. The company rented out theatre spaces, payed its actors a proper wage and financed musical arrangements. It was a success, at least until Duffer had a falling out with his music director. He had sacrificed his own theatre company in order to separate Robin and Kookla.

A knock at the door startled Duffer. He lifted himself off the couch, walked over to the door and opened it. A small Asian woman was standing in the hallway. She was wearing a house-coat and slippers.

'My side of the building has no running water,' she said.

'Oh,' replied Duffer. He noticed an empty plastic container in her hand.

'Can I trouble you for some water?' she asked.

'Of course,' he said. 'Come in.'

The woman entered his apartment.

'The kitchen's over there,' he gestured. Duffer waited by the door.

'I wouldn't have bothered you so late,' apologized the woman, 'but my daughter isn't feeling well.' She entered the kitchen and turned on the tap.

'I'm sorry to hear that,' he said. 'What seems to be the problem?'

'She sometimes has trouble breathing.'

The sudden gush of running water cleared Duffer's head. He listened to the sound and waited patiently. The water kept running. It ran for a long time. After a while Duffer had to finally ask, 'Is everything all right in there?' The woman didn't answer. 'Hello?' He raised his voice above the sound of the running water. There was still no reply.

Duffer entered the kitchen. The plastic water jug was overflowing and the woman was standing next to the sink and staring at the fridge. 'What's the matter?' he asked. The woman backed away from the fridge.

'It's you,' she said.

'What are you talking about?'

She pointed at the refrigerator door where her daughter's picture of the Boot Mover was posted. Duffer swallowed down an air bubble. 'I can't remember where I found that,' he trembled.

The woman moved away from Duffer and ran out of his apartment. She began to drum on all of the residents' doors.

'I found him … I found him … ' she shouted, 'the guy who moves the boots!'

The residents opened their doors and gathered as a group in the hallway. It sounded to Duffer like every person from every apartment was out there talking about him. He could hear their angry voices growing louder and getting closer.

'I'm getting closer,' Autumn said to himself. He could make out the form of the chestnut cabin. Its roof was covered with snow and its chimney threw off a few glowing embers. Autumn's foot grazed something soft on the path. He stopped and examined the object with the flashlight. It was a pink bladder-like thing in the snow.

'What the hell?' he said. Autumn touched it with the toe of his boot. It was spongy. He lifted the object from the snow and saw it was a plastic bag. The handles were tied in a rabbit's-ear knot. Autumn pulled off his gloves and untied the knot. He placed a bare hand inside the bag and withdrew a handful of human hair. It was Kookla's.

Autumn dropped the plastic bag and started running. The flashlight waved in all directions. When he arrived at the cabin the door was partly open. He entered and called out for Kookla. The light from a wood-burning stove cast a faint orange pall over two figures.

'Kookla,' he uttered.

Kookla was lying on the floor. Robin was kneeling beside her, cradling her body against his chest. Her arms were hanging lifeless by her sides. Robin's eyes were closed. He tried to sustain her by bracing her shoulders with his hands, but her shaved head was slack and sank toward the floor. There was a drop of blood on the floor underneath her.

'What have you done?' asked Autumn.

Robin lifted Kookla's body. He turned, faced Autumn and gently transferred Kookla into his arms. 'I loved her,' he said. 'This was the only way I could help her.'

Autumn carried her back to the ranger's cabin, stumbling through the snow under her weight. The ranger awakened, examined her wounds and shook his head in disbelief. He wrapped Kookla tightly in a blanket and secured her on a stretcher that was drawn behind his snowmobile. Within thirty minutes they were at the local hospital.

The ranger searched the emergency room for a doctor. The doctor, a silver-haired man in a lab coat, emerged from the on-call room. He was still half asleep and attempting to straighten his glasses. The two men discussed the situation. Autumn, light-headed and slightly off-balance, rested for a moment on the waiting room sofa. He listened to their conversation until things became very quiet around him. He looked up at the ceiling. His eyes were drawn to a water stain. The stain snaked the plaster and coiled at the base of a lighting fixture. The bowl of the fixture was half filled with a cloudy liquid. Autumn fell asleep.

'Are you all right?' asked the doctor.

'What?' mumbled Autumn.

'I asked if you're all right.'

Autumn forced himself into a sitting position. He stared at the waiting area and then at the doctor. It was early morning. His muscles were aching. The light from the admissions window was hurting his eyes. Autumn looked away from the doctor and put his head into his hands. His face was unshaven and scratchy. Autumn ran his fingers through his tangled hair. His body felt like a question mark that was crushed out of used tinfoil.

'Where am I?'

'You're in a hospital.'

Autumn remembered.

'Do you want me to examine you?'

'No,' he said. 'I'm all right.'

'That's fine,' said the doctor. 'Your friend is also doing quite well.'

'My friend?' repeated Autumn. 'Which one?'

'The female patient.'

'Do you mean Kookla?'

'Is that her name?'

Autumn nodded apprehensively. 'Is she alive?'

'Yes, she's alive, but she's unconscious right now.'

'Oh my god,' he muttered.

'You didn't know that she was alive?'

'I thought she was dead,' he answered. 'There was blood on her face … '

The doctor reached into his lab coat pocket and removed a plastic bag.

'Your friend Robin,' he asked, 'did he have a background in medicine?'

'Yes, I think he was in neurosurgery. But how do you know his name?'

'Robin turned himself in and gave this to the sheriff.' The doctor suspended the clear plastic bag in front of Autumn's face. Inside it was a stainless steel instrument. It had a long slender handle with a small rounded bud at one end. The bud of the instrument was bloodied. 'Do you know what this is?' he asked.

'No, I've never seen anything like it before.'

'This is an old surgical instrument,' the doctor explained. 'It's called a sounder. It hasn't been used in hospitals for over fifty years.'

'What's it used for?'

He tapped on his forehead, two fingers above the raised curve of his eyebrows. 'It's used for brushing away the connecting tissues of the frontal lobes.'

Autumn didn't say anything for a long time. The doctor returned the plastic bag and its contents to his pocket.

'We don't have the equipment in this facility to determine exactly how deep the instrument penetrated.'

'Will she recover?'

'She may not regain her eyesight,' he said. 'There may also be some neurological damage like flattening of emotional response or memory impairment. It's too early to tell.'

Autumn looked down. His boots made a puddle on the linoleum floor. 'What's going to happen to Kookla?' he asked.

'I'm arranging her transfer to another hospital.'

'And Robin?'

'He's in police custody. He'll have to undergo a seventy-two-hour psychiatric assessment to see if he's competent to stand trial. If he's found competent he'll be charged with attempted murder. Then again, according to the statement he submitted to the sheriff, Kookla might have co-operated with the assault. If that's the case, his charges might be reduced. Regardless, he'll be incarcerated for the rest of his life. Which reminds me – the police are here and they'd like to ask you some questions.'

'I'd like to see her first.'

'Not right now,' he advised. 'Wait here – you can see her after I've finished my rounds.' The doctor left Autumn and walked over to the nurses' station. He began to assemble his charts for the morning hand-over.

Autumn surveyed the emergency room. It was beginning to get busy. There was an elderly man on a stretcher breathing heavily and clutching his chest. An ambulance attendant held an oxygen mask to his face while his partner submitted a report to the triage nurse. A mother and daughter sat down on a seat facing Autumn. The little girl was holding a lion-shaped rag doll against her pulsing right ear. Soon afterwards a man with a cane limped over and sat down beside them.

Autumn left his seat and pushed unnoticed through the 'Hospital Staff Only' doors. He found several patient rooms on either side of a long narrow corridor. The floor had just been disinfected and the air smelled like ammonia. He noticed that one of the rooms had a chair outside the door. The chair was empty, which meant that the security guard was off duty.

Inside the room Autumn found Kookla resting on a hospital bed. Her eyes were bandaged shut underneath layers of white cotton gauze. A single drop of red blood spotted each orbit. She was wearing a hospital gown and was underneath a blanket. Her clothing had been placed inside a cardboard box labelled 'Evidence.' The room felt cold. The transparent bags on the IV pole dripped their medicines like thawing icicles. Their contents flowed into a plastic line that attached to Kookla's hand. A chart with the underlined word 'Forensics' was hanging by the door. Autumn approached the bedside and waited.

'Kookla,' he whispered, 'can you hear me?' He touched her hand gently and brushed against the plastic line in her vein. 'It's me … Autumn.' His eyes began to water. 'Duffer and Igor, they trusted that I would be there for you, that my love would be enough to keep you away from Robin.' He bent over the bedrail and kissed Kookla's wrist. 'I'm sorry,' he wept, 'but it wasn't enough. Duffer tried, before this, to separate you from Robin with the Medicine Show. But this also failed. Even Robin tried to keep away from you, but when he had learned how to separate your emotions from your memories, he returned.' Autumn stood up from the bed and wiped the tears from his eyes. He took one final look at Kookla. 'I love you,' he said and left the room.

On his way back to the waiting area, Autumn encountered a room he had mistaken for an exit. The walls were papered thick with colourful drawings. When he entered the room he realized that it was an old children's ward.

Autumn sat down on a small wooden chair and admired the drawings. There were hundreds of them on every wall. They overlapped like the pages of a calendar. He closed his eyes and tried to remember back to a time when he could produce the same kind of drawings. Autumn sat there for at least a half an hour. When he finally opened his eyes the doctor from the emergency room was standing in the doorway.

'So, there you are,' he said.

Autumn turned and faced the doctor.

'I've been looking for you.'

'I'm sorry,' said Autumn.

'You're not supposed to be in here.'

'I know,' he apologized.

The doctor stepped inside the room. 'I examined your friend Kookla.'

'How is she?'

'Well, she's regained consciousness,' he said, 'and she's responding appropriately.'

'She's responding?' cheered Autumn.

'Yes, but she keeps asking me the same question over and over again.'

'What does she ask?'

The doctor shook his head. '"Where's Robin? Where is he?"'

Acknowledgements

First and foremost I would like to thank Alana Wilcox of Coach House Books for her tremendous dedication to the novel and superb editing. I would also like to thank Karen Hansen for her encouragement and Carolynne Hew for her invaluable friendship. Finally, I must acknowledge the love and support of my family: Tzafi, Kenny and Miriam; my departed father, Jack; my partner, Evelyn, who inspired me to write; and my beautiful daughter, Hana.

About the Author

Ron Hotz is a family doctor with experience in emergency medicine and obstetrics. He is an assistant professor and lecturer at the University of Toronto with a special interest in the clinical training of medical residents. He and his partner, Evelyn, live in Toronto with their daughter, Hana. *The Animal Sciences* is his first novel.

Typeset in Bembo and printed and bound at the Coach House
on bpNichol Lane, 2003

Edited and designed by Alana Wilcox
Proofread by Gil Adamson
Cover art by Ron Hotz

Coach House Books
401 Huron Street (rear) on bpNichol Lane
Toronto, Ontario
M5S 2G5

1 800 367 6360

mail@chbooks.com
www.chbooks.com